AN
INCONVENIENT
WOMAN

Center Point
Large Print

**This Large Print Book carries the
Seal of Approval of N.A.V.H.**

AN INCONVENIENT WOMAN

STÉPHANIE BUELENS

CENTER POINT LARGE PRINT
THORNDIKE, MAINE

This book is dedicated to those who have the soul of a fighter, and who believe in genuine friendship.

To Paul Ward, William Larsen, Vittorio Carelli, for our shared tears, laughs, and endless fights for happiness; Rosheen and Raman Chawla, for their boundless generosity; and to my much unified family: my parents, Luc and Bernadette Buelens; my sister and brothers, Pauline, Grégoire, Matthieu; their wives, Cécile, and Florence; and their children, Mathis, Alexandre, Lola, Louison and Tom.

The whole world can become the enemy when you lose what you love.
        —Kristina McMorris
        Bridge of Scarlet Leaves

PROLOGUE

His power was in his arms, the muscles of his neck, the force of his legs, as he carried me out into the depths. Wrapped in his embrace, I felt as helpless as the sea beneath the moon. But I was not afraid.

Until he stopped and said, "Let go."

Instead I tightened my arms around his neck.

He pointed to the boat.

"Swim!"

It was too far, and the waves were high.

I held to him with all my might. It was useless. He unraveled my arms. They were no more than strands of twine.

"Swim," he repeated, and pushed me out into the current.

I went under, then surfaced.

"Swim to the boat, Claire," he ordered.

He was not to be disobeyed.

I swam.

The waves washed over me violently. There was something malicious in them. A hatred for my fear. I looked back, hoping that he might be swimming toward me. But he stayed in place, chest-deep in the roiling water.

A foaming crest sloshed over me. It filled my mouth with water. I gasped and coughed. My legs stopped pumping. My arms ceased thrashing. I sank heavily, like a stone.

Suddenly I saw a flash of light above me. Sun on the surface. I propelled myself toward it, clawing upward until I finally broke through. I was panting desperately. Ravenous for air.

I spun around, now certain that he must surely be coming to my rescue. But he remained where he had been.

The water seemed heavier. It had set its mind to swallow me. I couldn't let it. I kicked my legs, and with each thrust I pressed onward a little.

I pumped and pumped, moving forward inch by agonizing inch.

At last I made it to the boat.

I reached up, grabbed the gunwale. One more pull. I was almost safe. I drew in a deep breath. Readied myself for a final effort. One. Two. Three. Now!

Something gripped my still-submerged legs. I looked back into the water. His hands were on my ankles, tugging me down. I could see my father's head below the water.

Then there was a cry. "You okay?"

Another boat was closing on us, an old man at the helm. "You okay, sweetie?"

My father must have heard it, too. He released me, surfaced, and pretended to laugh.

But the truth was in his eyes.

PART I

CLAIRE

IN THE HALF-LIGHT of dawn, it comes to me in the vague, soft-focused form of a dream.

I know it's based on a memory, though as a vision it has a Hollywood feel. I watch it like a scene from a sweetly romantic movie. Something like *Robin and Marian*.

I'm standing in a broad green field.

I'm in my mid-twenties.

It's summer.

The light is bright and warm.

A wind sweeps over the undulating grass as a man presses close behind me.

I feel the warmth of his body and the feathery touch of his breath.

"Stand very still," he tells me.

He takes my hand and lifts it to the bow.

"Draw it toward me," he says.

He pulls back gently, my hand in his, and the bowstring tightens.

"Now hold," he says, when the string reaches almost the breaking point.

For a tense interval, everything balances at the tingling point of release.

Then he says, "Let go."

I do, and the arrow flies toward the waiting target.

Before it hits, I awaken and realize that it wasn't Robin Hood and Marian in a film.

It was Max and Claire in real life.

We weren't in a lush green field.

We were in the desert.

And it wasn't a bowstring I held. It was a gun.

Two hours later, I stare at my face in the bathroom mirror. It's a blur at first, but as the mist from the morning shower dissipates, my features become more distinct.

It's as if I'm rising slowly from a thick, watery depth. At last I break the surface.

There she is: Claire Fontaine.

Convincingly normal in every way.

Just another woman getting ready for work.

No one would guess.

After my shower, I put on my bathrobe, walk to my office, and turn on my computer.

I never cyberstalked Simon. But at the same time, I've kept a watchful eye on him. I have an alert on his name, and a few days ago I was notified of a marriage announcement.

I went online to confirm this, and there they were.

Simon, grinning triumphantly, certain that his latest prize is now in reach. Charlotte, his fiancée, unaware of what's coming.

Emma, her ten-year-old daughter.

I know he is going to do it again.

To remind myself of what he truly is, I type Simon's name in the search engine, then hit Images.

A wall of photographs pops onto the screen:

Simon at black-tie charity events.

On the golf course with celebrities, politicians, businessmen.

Simon giving civic awards and receiving them.

Simon the altruist, shovel in hand, breaking ground for an art center that will bear his name.

His wealth is on full display as well.

Simon at the door of his big house, leaning against a fancy car, at the helm of his yacht.

Was it this I fell for? Simon's big show?

If it was, I am even more to blame.

But there is no point in looking backward, in wishing I had seen his real face sooner.

I have to think of Emma.

Blond hair.

Blue eyes.

Innocent and trusting.

Simon's type in every way.

The phone rings as I am about to leave for my first client.

Simon's name appears on the caller ID.

It's a call I've been expecting, and yet I hesitate before answering it. Finally I respond with a clipped "Yes?"

"I can't believe you did this, Claire."

His voice is taut, controlled, everything about him kept in check.

In the background I hear the heavy slosh of water and immediately imagine him standing on the bow of his boat, dressed in that faux naval costume. Blue blazer with brass buttons. White pants and shoes. A cap with a gold insignia. The yacht he tellingly named *My Little Girl*.

"Claire? Are you there?"

When I don't answer, he turns lawyerly, a dispenser of sound advice. His tone is wise and patient. Who but a fool wouldn't listen to him?

"That letter was completely inappropriate, Claire. It's a groundless accusation. It always has been."

If I try to produce the kind of evidence he's used to and that he demands, the sort that's admissible in a court of law, I'll be on the defensive for the rest of the conversation. He will counter my every statement with a wily feint. It will frustrate and exhaust me. Leave me swirling with anger and powerlessness while he grins smugly at the other end of the line.

Some women act on their rage. They take a tire iron to their husband's car. They crack its windshield and shatter its headlights and beat its metal skin.

If a woman's fury could be soothed so easily, there'd be no cars on the road.

Simon, the chameleon, now transforms himself into a psychologist. The kind we see on television: helpful, solicitous, dripping with sympathy and understanding.

He talks about my "corrosive guilt," my "trust issues," my "outrageous suspicions."

Then he moves on to our life together.

He is sorry it ended as it did, brought low by my own "dark history," by which he means that my father tried to drown me. A story he obviously doesn't believe and probably mocks behind my back: *Claire's first delusion.*

Or does he bother to talk behind my back?

Am I even worth his ridicule?

"I still care about you," he says. "I really do."

I know this isn't true. Divorce is an eraser.

Unfortunately, I haven't been erased enough.

Like a stubborn stain, I have reappeared.

"Please, Claire, let's just call this an unfortunate episode."

I hear him, but I can't help imagining what might have been. My daughter, Melody, at twenty-one, just graduating from college. In this alternative future, she is telling me not to worry: "Oh, Mom, you are *so SM.*" Texting shorthand: Single Mom. Now the scene shifts into the past and she is a girl of eight, playing in the sea. Light glitters on the water. She calls these flashes "diamonds."

I know that this is an odd twist of mind, this

moving back and forth in time, from what was to what might have been. There are occasions when I "remember" the future as if it has already happened, past and future blending like the colors on an artist's palette. At such moments it is only the present that seems unreal.

For Simon, this is just another symptom of my derangement. A mind-set he can use to build his case against me.

But I can't help giving Melody a future, even if it's only imagined.

I see her again. Playing in the pool, Max teaching her how to swim. All of us laughing. Melody on a pony, Max holding the reins. The storied holidays sweep by: Melody opening her Christmas presents, or at a large Thanksgiving table, Max carving the traditional turkey.

Max, my husband.

Melody, my daughter.

Once I had a family.

"Can we do that, Claire?" Simon asks. "Can we just say that you . . . had a little breakdown?"

Simon, the long-suffering and forgiving friend.

When again I don't answer, he releases a dramatic, world-weary sigh. "This silent treatment is childish. Absolutely childish."

He is now the frustrated father.

How many disguises does he have?

Ava considers men little boys who rush toward a cliff. They are always certain that they won't go over the edge. Simon has this kind of self-assurance.

"Are you listening to me, Claire?"

His voice is solicitous, kindly. You'd think he was my guardian angel. It reminds me of my father's voice. They both pretend to feel sorry for me and regret that I am a victim of sinister delusions. I could be happy, they insist, if I would just shuffle off these malicious visions. *Move on* is their shared mantra. *Forget the past. Especially the parts you've only concocted.*

There are times when their lips seem poised at my ears.

Whispering incessantly, *None of it is true.*

Sometimes I press my hands against my ears to silence them.

Like a woman who is truly crazy.

Once or twice I have even screamed.

Silently.

Only in my mind.

No one hears.

"I can't let you do this again, Claire," Simon tells me. "Not to me or yourself. And certainly not to Charlotte or Emma."

At last his best role emerges: Simon as the benevolent protector. A man who never thinks of himself. It is always someone else he is trying to protect. Once it was me and Melody. Now it is Charlotte and Emma. It will always be someone. And it will always be a lie.

"Please remember what happened last time," he adds.

We finally arrive at where such exchanges always end: a threat.

He's made it subtle and indirect, but I feel it like a slap.

I've had enough.

"Do you remember how Melody looked?" I ask him coldly.

"It was an accident, Claire. She got in a boat. The sea was turbulent, and it overturned."

"And why did she get in that boat, Simon?"

Simon is exasperated.

The answer to that question is one he won't acknowledge.

"I have a right to be happy," he says firmly, almost nobly, like a man defending a sacred document. "I won't let you stand in my way."

He hangs up.

I feel like a tuning fork struck hard. Still vibrating.

I put down my phone, walk into the yard, and let the morning sun pour over me. It's hot and dry. In its bright light, my twitching nerves grow still.

Abruptly I feel exposed, an easy target.

As vulnerable as a deer in an open field.

I walk back into the house, and for distraction turn on the television.

"The body of a girl was found floating this

morning among the pylons of Santa Monica Pier."

A girl in the water.

I think of Melody swirling in the waves.

It's a powerful connection.

A sisterhood of the drowned.

The screen shows policemen on the beach, standing over a black body bag.

"The victim has not been identified, and her cause of death has not yet been determined."

Years ago, when I was studying art history in Paris, I read about the body of another girl. A teenager. Floating in the Seine. No one knew who she was, so they called her "*L'Inconnue,*" the Unknown. A photograph of her death mask became a hot item among the city's artists. They framed it and hung it in their studios. German girls modeled their looks on her. She became a romantic ideal.

I sweep into an invented future. Melody is now sixteen, reading in her room. A poster of *L'Inconnue* is thumbtacked to her wall. Along with one of Amy Winehouse.

I finish dressing. Before leaving, I give myself a quick once-over to make sure everything is properly in place before heading to my first client. My earrings are modest, with a short dangle. My shoes are low-heeled. My blouse is silk, light pink. My skirt is black and falls just above the knee. I use very little makeup and a pale lipstick with a touch of gloss. No visible bra strap or panty line. Nothing provocative.

"Anyone having information concerning this girl should contact the Los Angeles Police Department at the following tip line."

I reach for one of my notebooks and write down the number on the screen. I have no idea why I do this. I don't know the girl in the water. And besides, she's dead. I can't save her. Perhaps I write the number because I've been watching movies on a new cable network called Femme Fatale. Last night's movie began with a woman in a raincoat running from an oncoming car.

Watching this scene, I was reminded of three days before, when I decided to write to Simon. The fear I'd felt as I'd written that single, chilling line:

I won't let you do it again.

In noir films, the women are brave and smart. They know how to move and talk and get out of a tight spot. They are always one step ahead of whoever is pursuing them.

It will be much harder to stay ahead of Simon.

I hear his voice in my head: *I won't let you stand in my way.*

He has the means to back up his threats. Money. Influence. He is a prominent lawyer, with important clients. An officer of the court. All the powers that be are on his side.

I have only myself.

On the way to my car, I see Mr. Cohen waving at me from the adjoining yard. He calls me his "adopted daughter" and advises me on the Big Questions. His nurse often rolls him out in the morning, then goes back inside to tidy up. Today he looks lonely, isolated, a castaway marooned on his wheelchair island. His wife died many years ago, and his only son was killed in Iraq. He is a great lover of the classics, particularly the Greeks. He says that he is like Creon in *Antigone*: schooled by sorrow.

Perhaps I am, too.

After we chat awhile, he says, "You look like you're under strain, Claire. Anything in particular?"

I tell him it's an item in the morning news, the drowned girl.

He looks at me sympathetically.

I know what he's thinking. He's concerned that this latest drowning has brought it all back. The rain. The wind-tossed sea. The heaving boat. Melody's body in the water.

I see myself reflected in his eyes, *Claire on the brink.*

I understand his concern.

He's no doubt seen women like me before.

Tense. Strained. At loose ends. Perhaps falling apart.

He assumes such women are capable of anything.

He may be right.

I go to my car, insert the key, and fire the engine.

As I back out of my driveway, I catch my eyes in the mirror. They look cold, fierce, steely.

I'm frightened by them.

Mr. Cohen is right.

Anything.

2.

On the way to my first client, I pass the auction house where I once worked. I never go there, because the Claire my colleagues and customers knew then—talkative, outgoing, funny—is not the Claire I am now, wound tight, on edge, forever on guard, an LA version of the madwoman in the attic.

Melody was four years old when I first took her to the auction house. Max went with us that day. We strolled through rooms of paintings. Melody was alert and eager. She was fascinated by a collection dubbed "Fantasies." They presented a whimsical world of floating faces, eyes bulging from trees, boats with butterfly sails. Everything in them was weird and topsy-turvy. Melody found them funny.

At one point she rode happily on Max's shoulders. Together in that way, they appeared as one body, the two of them melded, one form seamlessly rising from the other. This physical representation of their closeness seemed equally fantastical to me, father and daughter bound in a way that was beautifully surreal.

Now I make my living teaching French, the language I learned from my mother.

Her name was Martine. She was Parisian in every way a woman could be. Elegant and sophisticated, with a finely tuned intelligence. She adored her native language and spoke it beautifully. It rolled off her tongue like music, each word a rich and subtle note.

I remember sitting on her lap, listening delightedly as she repeated the numbers, the days of the week, the seasons.

It was like hearing her sing.

At night, when she tucked me in, she'd say, *A demain. Je t'aime très fort. Bonne nuit.*

Her voice transformed these ordinary phrases into a lullaby.

She died when I was seven, leaving my father to pursue another woman and me to continue with the language she'd taught me to love, every word a memory of her.

I know that for some of my clients, French is a fantasy language, the gateway to a different and far better life. They imagine moving to Paris. City of Light. City of romance. They would sip wine in a bistro. Talk about art. Find a love that stops time and never knows betrayal.

If it were that simple, why would anyone live anywhere else?

I've learned that a language is a way of confirming who you really are and what you really feel. From time to time I would say *Je t'aime* to Max, and though he didn't speak French, he knew what "I love you" meant.

I said the same to Simon during our first years together, as we both watched Melody mature.

My life is different now.

To Simon I have only one thing to say: *Je vais me battre.*

It's a defiant declaration, because I know he wants me to surrender to his power and his threats.

What he wants is for me to disappear, one way or the other.

His dream is that I will let him do whatever he wishes.

I won't do that.

Je vais me battre.

I'm going to fight.

I started my new life as a French teacher with a flyer. In it, I'd planned to assure prospective students that I would pattern my lessons to their needs, provide a relaxing atmosphere, be flexible with regard to time and place.

My friend Ava warned me that men would take *flexible* the wrong way. Also *relaxing.*

"Everything turns them on," she said.

I took her warning seriously, and thus my flyer reads: *Claire Fontaine, French Teacher,* with no mention of flexibility or relaxation.

I include my email address and my phone

number, but I don't reveal my actual address, though I understand that, given access to the internet, anyone can find it. I do the same for my posts on Thumbtack and Craigslist and other online job sites.

As I drive, I try to focus on the time when I wasn't watchful or distrusting, when the way ahead didn't seem fraught with danger or the past an accusation.

I remember when I was a student in Paris, walking those fabled boulevards, going to museums, speaking a language that made me feel at home. It was my city of refuge, beyond the reach of childhood terror. While there, I read a line from a Greek philosopher whose name I no longer recall. *We don't do what we want,* he wrote, *we do what we can't avoid.* In Paris, the grim nature of that statement didn't strike me as either true or inevitable.

Now it does.

Today I'm headed for Playa Vista. I drive a white PT Cruiser that spends a lot of time being repaired. It's like an old body. Wheezing. Leaking. Breaking down. Ava laughed when she first saw it. She called it a "loser's car." And yet I feel a strange closeness to things that shake and rattle, that have been bumped and battered but still manage to hold together.

Ting.

I keep driving, trying to ignore my message alert. It's probably only a client canceling a class. Or a new contact looking for a French teacher. But in the wake of Simon's threat, this *ting* now comes to me as a disquieting intrusion.

I pull over, snap my phone from its dashboard clamp.

The message is from someone named Phil.

He has seen my profile on OkCupid, the matching service I signed up with one evening when the loneliness was just too much.

U seem like an interesting person. And U speak French. Wow!!!! U say U R 42, but U look younger. Wood U like 2 Meat?

I know that Ava would counter with a hard, sarcastic *Know, Eye Wood Knot.*

What would be the point of such derision? It would only provoke a nasty response. Ava enjoys goading men in this way. She often shows me their heated retorts to the mocking rejections she hurls back at them. Inevitably, tempers rise. Texts shoot through cyberspace like flaming arrows.

Ava finds this game of escalating insult quite amusing.

I see only how quickly hurt turns to anger in the men she antagonizes.

So I choose a gentler answer: *Soon leaving LA, but thank you.*

I have no such plan, of course.

And yet I imagine myself rushing toward a

hastily packed car, racing for the freeway in the middle of the night. The air around me brightens as another car closes in from behind. Am I already a woman in full flight?

Is it this thought that causes me to notice the SUV that suddenly pulls in behind me?

It's black and very large, almost tanklike. As I head down Sunset, it draws closer, then holds back in a strange rhythm, like a dance. It's never near enough for me to get a look at the driver, and there is no front license plate. I would have to get behind it to read those numbers, but each time I slow to let the SUV go ahead of me, it pulls back.

Is the driver carefully keeping his distance, or is it only the normal ebb and flow of traffic?

Just once, at a light, it pulls up alongside, but its side windows are darkly tinted.

I can't see the driver, but I visualize his face. Grim. Calculating. Recording my features, studying his target.

The word seems appropriate.

A moving target.

When the light turns, I accelerate, then make a quick, almost violent turn onto the next side street. In my rearview mirror I watch the SUV sweep through the intersection.

I tighten my grip on the wheel and try to convince myself that the driver of the SUV is just another motorist. And yet, as I make a U-turn and head back toward my usual route, I continually check my mirrors. At each cross street I glance left and right, expecting to see the same black SUV lurking at the curb, ready to renew its pursuit, its driver accustomed to such simple evasive maneuvers as mine.

When I don't see it, I let myself imagine that the driver really was one of Simon's minions.

I am pleased and proud that I have eluded him.

Just like the women in noir films.

I glance at my face in the mirror.

To my surprise, I'm smiling.

I continue down Sunset. There is no further sign of the black SUV.

My brief instant of exhilaration has passed.

I'm again tense and vigilant when I arrive at my client's apartment a few minutes later.

Her name is Mia. She is thirty-one years old. Small, with something vaguely fragile about her even though she is a corporate lawyer. She has recently acquired a French boyfriend. She is learning the language in preparation for meeting his parents.

"Hi," she says as she opens the door.

She steps back to let me in.

"Coffee?"

"No, thank you."

The apartment is large, with a generous amount of sunlight flowing through two skylights. She has decorated it in bright colors, but the pouring light bleeds away their vibrancy, so that the room looks old and faded. The corpse of a dance hall.

We sit in her office. Mia has her usual mug of coffee, white with big red letters: I CONTROL THE UNIVERSE.

"I'm not going until December now," she says.

She means that Remi, her boyfriend, has decided to delay their trip to France, thus putting her target date for learning French six months further off.

Mia offers her edgy smile. "I'll have more time to learn."

She has resisted our starting with the most basic vocabulary. She prefers to focus on what she calls the "love words." Only the romantic phrases appeal to her. The French of lovers.

So instead of teaching her to tell time or order food or get directions, I concentrate on the warm, starry-eyed expressions she wants to learn.

"*Embrasse-moi. Enlace-moi. Aime-moi,*" I say very slowly. Kiss me. Hold me. Love me.

While Mia repeats the French haltingly, I find myself recalling my first meeting with Simon. Melody was ten. We were at LACMA. Melody was walking among the lampposts outside the museum. Simon was standing nearby. He seemed unsure of whether he should approach me, but in the end he made his way over to where I stood.

"Your daughter?" he asked.

"Yes."

His smile was warm, beckoning. A smile that could be trusted.

"She'll be a beautiful woman." His eyes drifted over to me. "Like her mother."

Delivered in that way, I should have read it as a hokey line. And yet he seemed sincere. As if we were at the beginning of a great romance.

Simon the lonely man in search of love.

The first of his many masks.

I recall the rose petals he placed on my pillow, along with an occasional French chocolate.

How false all of that seems to me now.

Like the staging of a house for sale.

So much so that when Mia asks for an appropriate phrase with regard to falling in love, only one answer occurs to me:

Fais attention.

Be careful.

3.

It's noon by the time I meet Ava at Little Next Door in West Hollywood. She's a transplanted New Yorker. Utterly contemptuous of LA. She calls it "empty," "brain-dead." A city so vacuous she once circulated a mock online petition to take away its zip code.

We meet for lunch every Monday, and during most of that time together we talk like veterans of what she still calls "the war between the sexes." Each of us has been wounded, but in different campaigns. Her divorce was long and brutal, though she claims to have come through it triumphantly. *I got the mine, he got the shaft,* was her later mantra. She had it made into a bumper sticker and pasted it to her flashy new Audi.

She has said many times that she never found the "love of her life." She suspects that I did in Max, and she is right. He was kind, loving, patient, and understanding. He had all the big-ticket virtues. Never more than in his long dying. Melody was only five during that final year, and each time I took her to him, his pain and anguish fell away, and he seemed, for all his sorrow, for all that he was losing, very grateful for what he had.

And so was I.

Despite the long, hopeless treatment, his wasting away.

What I recalled in the following years was how gracefully he had died, how tender he had remained. At the end he'd had just enough strength to whisper, "You are very kind" to a hospice nurse.

They were his last words.

It's comforting to remember his tenderness and generosity.

But I also know how profoundly disappointing he would find what I did on Simon's boat that night.

"What's new, Claire?" Ava asks brightly.

Before I can answer, I notice a man take a seat at a table not far away. He is tall, powerfully built, wearing dark glasses. His body looks hard, muscular. A wrestler disguised as a businessman. I envision him earlier behind the wheel of that black SUV. Is he now quietly amused by how cleverly he gave me the false illusion of having escaped him?

I force myself to look away and return my attention to Ava. By then I've forgotten her question.

"What?" I ask. "What did you say?"

Ava looks at me oddly. "Are you okay?"

"Yes. You asked me something?"

"I asked you if anything is new," Ava says.

I don't want to tell her about Simon. Either my letter or his call. She is on my side, but at the same time, the specter of my confronting Simon again frightens her. He is a hornet's nest I shouldn't kick over. She considers any effort to stand in his way to be a lost cause.

"No, nothing new," I tell her.

"Okay, well, before we get into anything else and I forget it, I want to give you this."

She takes a business card from her purse and hands it to me.

"He came into my office just this morning. We talked. It turns out he's interested in learning French."

I look at the card: *Ray Patrick.*

The card says that Ray owns an art gallery in Melrose. It gives no indication of the sort of art he prefers. I suspect that its off-white walls hold canvases of California Impressionism.

Seascapes.

The desert.

Sailboats resting languidly in the marina.

"I gave him one of your flyers," Ava tells me. "Expect a call."

She adds a small, collusive wink.

"You have art in common."

I don't address my friend's relentless match-making. Despite her confrontational attitude toward men, she still considers a woman with no one in her life somewhat pathetic. I know that in her eyes I'm a bit shaky and in need of repair. Like my PT Cruiser.

"Just don't be too bookish, Claire," Ava says, half scolding, half pleading, in every way nudging me toward a less solitary life.

She reaches over and touches my hand.

"Let the poor guy get to know you first. Think love, Claire, not books."

I think of a book I recently read. It was about falling in love. The author is trying to find the essential element that defines this act. It is not fulfillment of desire or the joy of discovering your missing half. It doesn't provide warmth or comfort or any sense of permanence. Just the opposite, in fact. The core of falling in love, he says, is jeopardy. When you fall in love, you place your heart and soul on a single number and spin the wheel. Reading this, I'd felt only how fully I'd lost my taste for gambling.

I reluctantly glance over at the man in the business suit. He has not taken off his sunglasses. He is studying the menu. Or at least pretending to study it. I notice that at times he seems to be looking over it. At me? I can't be sure, and yet I feel a vague tightness all over, my skin drawing in, as if I'm becoming my own straitjacket.

To avoid this disturbing sensation, I look at Ray Patrick's card, then quickly pocket it as the waiter steps up.

I choose the cheese plate, Ava the foie gras.

She also orders a Sauternes. I have my usual sparkling wine.

"Let's start again," Ava says. "Anything new in your life?"

"They found a girl floating near the pier this morning. I saw it on the news before I left the house."

Something in Ava's eyes suggests I've tripped an alarm.

"I never watch the news," she says.

The implication is that I should avoid this, too. Perhaps she thinks my mind is too frail to confront the cruel realities of life.

"It's always something depressing," she adds. "War. Car accidents. Disturbing."

"They're always finding them, aren't they?" I tell her. "Murdered women."

In photographs they look haphazardly discarded.

Tossed into ditches.

Dragged into woods.

Dredged up from lakes and rivers and canals.

Human litter.

"Who says this girl was murdered?" Ava asks. "Maybe she slipped. Maybe she jumped. You always go to the dark side, Claire."

She reaches for her glass.

"You've got to stop thinking about stuff like that."

"Simon's getting married," I tell her.

"Ex-husbands always do," Ava says with a sardonic laugh. "To someone younger, prettier. Some airhead dumb enough to worship them. It's how they get even."

"His fiancée has a little girl named Emma. She's ten years old. That's the same age as Melody when I met him."

Ava looks at me apprehensively.

"Don't go there, Claire."

"There was a picture of them all together," I continue determinedly.

"A picture?"

"I saw it online."

"Online? You're . . . spying on him?"

"I wouldn't call it that."

"No? Checking on someone online is spying, Claire. What else would you call it?"

Before I can answer, she rushes ahead.

"Why are you doing that? What does it get you? For God's sake, move on with your life. There's nothing you can do about Simon. You took him on once. Remember what it got you? You were arrested, Claire. Arrested! You want that to happen again?"

"No, I don't. But how can I ignore the fact that Emma looks exactly like Melody when she was ten? Am I supposed to just close my eyes and forget it?"

I lean forward.

"Everything about her is the same, Ava," I say

insistently. "The color of her eyes. Her hair. The shape of her body. Everything."

My voice is louder than I mean it to be, my tone more frenzied. A few people glance over at me, then, as if unsettled by what they see, return to their food and companions.

Ava takes a quick sip from her glass.

I ease back in my chair and try to calm myself.

"I know what he's going to do, Ava," I tell her in a much quieter voice. Controlled. Reserved. Like a woman who has given her soul a sedative.

"You don't have any proof, Claire," Ava reminds me in a much less combative tone.

She is trying to lower the volume, cool the fire in me.

"Not a shred of proof," she adds.

She's right, at least technically. I have no proof of what Simon is going to do. But I know the man behind his collection of poses. I have seen his real face. If I could paint his portrait with the colors of the truth, he would have horns and fangs.

Ava will understand none of this, of course, and so I make no further argument.

The food arrives. It looks very French, each plate presented with a little dash of style.

When I was six, my mother and I went to Paris together to visit my grandparents. They had lived in the city all their lives, seen it through its most melancholy days. My great-grandmother had waved goodbye as my great-grandfather boarded the train that would take him to the fiery slaughter of Verdun. Twenty years later my grandparents had mutely watched, heartbroken, as German troops paraded down the Champs-Elysées. *It is the City of Light,* my grandmother once said, *but it is also the City of Tears.*

My mother was already dying when we made our last visit to Paris. The trip was hard for her, but she'd wanted us to share the city one last time and so she'd borne the pain and the exhaustion with a heroic resolution. With every cough and every wince, I'd admired her more.

While we were there, she took me to a bakery where they made small marzipan peaches. She pointed out how the leaves on each peach were delicately veined and the flesh glowed with a faint red blush. At base the peaches were composed of a simple paste made of almonds, sugar, and water, but somehow the confectioners had made them live.

"It's these little touches of beauty that make life worth living, Claire," she told me.

When Melody was the same age, we went to Paris to visit my grandparents.

While there, I took her to the same shop, showed her the same marzipan peaches, and repeated the same words to her that my mother had said to me.

This is still one of the dearest of my memories,

but even the most tender moments of my past now seem to have occurred in a different, far less tender world.

I pull myself back to the present, to what I know Simon is going to do.

"I have all the proof I need," I tell Ava in a way that makes it clear that I want to drop the subject.

Ava obviously prefers to drop it, too. "Anyway, the point is to make yourself available again," she tells me.

"Available to what?"

She smiles. "Love, stupid."

I think of Phil.

His OkCupid message was less silly than those of the men who send pictures of themselves in front of sparkling blue swimming pools, shirtless, showing off their bodies. In the world of gooney-bird courtship display, Phil kept his plumage to a minimum.

"Claire, you're young. You're attractive. You're clever. You speak French, which is probably a huge turn-on, right?"

I look at her doubtfully.

"At least it makes you seem romantic," she says.

I offer another questioning look.

Ava waves her hand.

"What I'm saying is that you have everything to offer. So turn the page. Open a new chapter. End of story."

I understand what she wants me to do, but I can't put what I know in a bottle and toss it overboard.

Instead I feel myself drawn back into the darkness, back to Simon on the phone.

I glance toward the man in the sunglasses.

He is gone.

After lunch with Ava, I have a half hour to kill before my next client. I sit in my car and read. The book is about the Muses. I like Thalia, the muse of comedy. And Clio, the muse of history. It is Mneme, the inventor of language, who touches me. The saddest of the Muses, haunted as she is by memory.

Once more I sink back in time.

I am in the second-floor bedroom I share with Simon. Standing at the window, looking down at the pool. Melody is thirteen. She is doing laps, her long white legs churning the water. Simon is in a lounge chair, wrapped in a white robe, his initials woven with gold thread. His hands are at his sides, but as he watches Melody from the far side of the pool, one of them crawls up his thigh and into his lap. His fingers are slipping inside his robe when he glimpses me in the window, pulls his hand away, and waves to me broadly, sporting a huge smile.

It astonishes me that I ever believed in that smile.

Or in his summoning wave.

How could I have been so blind?

How could I have sensed nothing in the furtive way his fingers inched beneath his robe?

Nor ever guessed the perverse turn of his mind?

Now I'm certain that at that very instant he was in the grip of an obscene pleasure. I see his creepiness in every memory of his taking Melody's hand. I see it in the way he draped his arm over her shoulder and held her waist as he taught her to dance. The shadow of his desire darkens every recollection of them together.

I am reliving all this when a *ting* alerts me to a text.

It's from Mehdi, who has taken six classes so far. He has sent me a picture of himself wearing a Burger King crown: *See, I told you that I am the King of Persia.*

Actually he's a florist with several high-end shops around Los Angeles. He is forty-six, divorced, with a six-year-old son. His wife cheated on him. His pride was devastated. He is working, he says, to rebuild his self-esteem. He is doing this by going to the gym. Doing upper body. Swinging on the parallel bars. He sends videos of himself doing these things. I am supposed to be impressed by his strength. Instead I see only a fly in a jar, banging against the glass.

I return to my book. The author is trying to make his work more accessible by mentioning "modern muses." For the modern muse of music, he chooses Yoko Ono. As I read, I find myself not caring much about her. Instead I am moved by May Pang, Lennon's mistress. They were together for eighteen months. John never called it more than his "lost weekend."

How is it possible for lovers to conceive of time so differently?

Is it the same with Simon and me?

That while I fear I may have little time left to do what I must, he is sure he has forever to carry out his scheme?

I read a few minutes longer, then close the book. But I can't stop myself from looking up and down the street. I feel the corrosive nature of this impulse, this slide into seeing everything as somehow threatening. Everyone working for Simon. The people on the street. The people in their cars. That man over there, raking the yard. When he stops and looks at me, I freeze. It is almost as if I believe him to be Simon in yet another of his forms. Camouflaged in khaki, his face carefully hidden beneath a wide-brimmed hat.

4.

Dominic is my next client. He is sixteen. His parents feel that he will, as his father tells me, "always sink to the lowest common denominator." Dominic is being forced to learn French as a "cultural enhancement." He does his lessons because he has no choice. I know that his only passion is for the video game he plays, during which he kills "Entities" in paroxysms of slaughter he labors to describe to me in French.

During these exchanges I fear the budding psychopath.

"In French," he once asked me, "how do you say 'to gut'?"

After Dominic, Mehdi is almost a relief.

Almost.

He smiles brightly as he opens the door. "Ah, my queen."

I step into his foyer, then go a few steps farther before I turn, holding my bag like a shield against my chest.

"Please come to the dining room," Mehdi says. "I have prepared for us a . . . *repas*."

"I've already eaten," I tell him.

"But I made it special. Food for the queen."

His smile flips like a small worm.

"Or should I say *la reine*?"

During our first classes, Mehdi followed the lessons well. However, over the last couple of weeks he has decided to play my life coach. He says that I need to "eat healthy," sleep more, relax in the evening, get a massage. In long texts written at odd hours, he offers his psychological counseling. I must be strong, trust myself, and "open up to others," as he wrote—at three a.m.—last Tuesday.

He escorts me into the dining room, where he has arranged various pastries, along with little bowls of loose nuts and dried fruits.

He displays these offerings like a billboard. With Mehdi, everything is a form of presenting himself in a big, bright light, like the ones that sweep the Hollywood sky on the night of a premiere. He is not only the star of his own blockbuster movie, he is the only actor in it.

"Please," he says as he points to a chair.

He is a small man. A little stocky. Going bald. But there is a compact forcefulness about him. He talks aggressively. Moves in quick steps. His internal engine is always racing.

Once again I tell him that I have already eaten.

"Okay." He is a bit crestfallen now. "We start." He motions toward the table. "We can work here, yes?"

The table has a glass top, and I wonder if this, more than the *repas*, is part of his plan. A table he can see through. I take my seat, careful to arrange myself as modestly as possible. Even so, he glances at my legs as I sit down.

"Nice. You look nice."

He says it gently, but in this otherwise mild compliment there is the suggestion of something tightly wound, of barely controlled impulses. I imagine him as a child, snatching candy from another kid, then forced to give it back.

I draw a book from my bag and place it strategically on the table, blocking any view of my legs.

"Someday I will take you to the beach at Caicos," Mehdi says. "We will bask in the sun with chilled glasses of champagne. The sand is like white powder. Just Claire and Mehdi, eh?"

I show no interest in this proposal and simply continue the class for the next hour.

Mehdi says nothing more about the beautiful beaches of Caicos.

As I am leaving, he smiles. "Maybe we could meet twice a week now?"

I need the money, yet I buy time before deciding. "I'll check my schedule and let you know."

With that, I head for my car, get in, and drive away. I am halfway to my next client when I hear the *ting* of a text. It is from Mehdi, a photograph of himself wearing a long Iranian robe: *Perhaps you will be my queen.*

It is only a text message, but it is invasive, like an unwanted touch.

I want to tell Mehdi to go away. I would like to say it firmly: *Back off!*

But a chorus of monthly bills stops me.

"Keep quiet," says my rent.

"Not so fast," says my credit card.

And yet each time I hesitate, I feel some small part of myself fall away, like flecks from a self-portrait—a shard of self-respect, a fleck of dignity, the vivid colors of myself peeling away or fading into a blur.

5.

It's nearly nine in the evening when I get back home.

I go into the kitchen, make a dinner of pasta and roasted vegetables. The empty chair across from me is like an accusation. Where Melody would have sat.

Time sweeps me into the future, and I imagine her sitting with a husband at her side, a child on her lap.

Then the flow of my mind takes me back to my own wedding day.

It was a simple courthouse affair; Max and I were married by a local judge in his chambers.

The lack of grand display had gone perfectly with the beautiful simplicity of the vows.

To have and to hold.
For better or for worse.
For richer or poorer.
In sickness and in health.
From this day forward.
Till death do us part.

When this memory fades, another seizes me like a hand out of the dark. Simon was resplendent in his morning coat; I was gloriously enveloped in an expensive gown.

The big church with the vaulted ceiling.

The huge sprays of flowers perfuming the air.

A classical quartet playing Mozart while Simon's big-name friends strolled in and took their seats.

Almost as a way of fleeing that ostentatious ceremony, I walk into the living room, part the curtains, and peer out into the night.

What I am looking for?

Simon's accomplices?

I tell myself that these fears are irrational, and yet when the phone rings, I startle.

It rings again.

Then again.

I still don't respond, though I know I should.

Finally, on the fifth ring, I answer it.

It's Ray Patrick, the man Ava mentioned as a prospective client.

"I'm interested in learning French," he tells me. "Your friend Ava gave me your name." He pauses, then adds, "I go to France quite often on business. I was hoping to get a bit more proficient in the language."

I ask him if he speaks French at all.

He replies that he does not.

"Well, I can say *oui* and *non*," he adds.

I give him my rate, which is $50 an hour.

"That's fine," Ray Patrick says. "Where do you want to meet?"

"Is there a Starbucks near you?"

"I can come to the one on Beverly Drive."

We agree to meet there the following afternoon.

Before I can hang up, he says, "I know you studied art. I thought you might like to take a look at my gallery. The website, I mean. It's rpgallery.com. I'd love to know what you think."

"Okay, I'll take a look."

I go to my computer, type in the name. Ray Patrick's gallery is lovely and well ordered, with a surprising variety of styles. I do a virtual tour, make some notes, record a few words he might find useful when speaking to artists or gallery owners in France.

Then I turn off the computer, glance at the clock, and quickly go to my car.

For the last few months I have been mentoring a young woman named Destiny. She lives in an apartment a few blocks from the senior center where we meet once a week.

She has told me little of her background, save that she is from "the sticks," by which she means a small town in the Midwest. Predictably, there are dark suggestions of a troubled childhood but few details. She chooses to speak mostly of the future, broad dreams of owning a clothing store or a horse farm or, at our last meeting, a catering service, because she'd recently met a woman who had one, and so why not?

Through she doesn't like to talk about her past because it "drags her down," I've learned that she has an older brother who was continually bullying her and a younger sister who was "just a little bitch." She has never told me their names or their whereabouts and seems to have no interest in ever seeing either of them again.

She feels pretty much the same about her parents. She has said only, "Maybe they're dead. Maybe they're alive. Either way, I don't care."

This doesn't strike me as a false front. She honestly appears to have no feeling for them at all.

From various offhand remarks of hers, I've gathered that she was not a good student, found it difficult to overcome even the smallest obstacles, and had a tendency to take the easy way out.

Briefly, she thought about joining the military, but the mental and physical rigors of training to be a soldier were too much for her to tackle.

Her most harrowing story is of the time she barely escaped a man who'd picked her up, taken her to his house, then tried to rape her. She has spoken of this only once. The man was "old," she said, *old* being defined as "over forty."

For a few weeks, Destiny was homeless. After her boyfriend disappeared, she wandered the streets, sleeping wherever she found shelter. At some point she made her way to Venice Beach, where she was spotted by a social worker.

Beyond the sketchy and perhaps somewhat unreliable history, she remains pretty much a blank.

She is waiting for me in a room the center provides for this purpose. Her hair is short, black, spiky. It looks as if it were cut by a weed eater. She has tattoos on her back, shoulders, and arms. She says she has them in other places as well. The visible ones are snakes and vines, along with the initials *TW* in satanic script. TW is Time Warp, the only name she has for her long-lost boyfriend. There are small puncture holes in her nose, ears, and lips. The metal studs that used to fill them have been removed because they "freaked people out" at 24/7, the eatery where she currently works as a waitress.

There are occasions during my conversations with Destiny when I imagine Melody as a runaway, talking to a woman who is not her mother about a life that has gone seriously awry. Even such a future might have been redeemed. She might have passed through a rough stage but found her footing again. This is the precious gift that was taken from my daughter, simply the opportunity to have overcome whatever obstacles she encountered in order to become whatever she'd hoped to be.

"Hi," Destiny says with an eager wave that may or may not be entirely sincere.

Tonight we talk about her job. It's going well, she says. Except for another young woman at 24/7. This girl is named Muriel. There is no love lost between them. The issue is envy. Destiny has a good figure. Muriel is overweight. Destiny can remember who gets what when she serves. Muriel is always giving soup to someone who ordered a burger and vice versa. Destiny is regularly hit on. No one pays any attention to Muriel.

"Muriel's fat. How is that my fault?"

There is a pause before she adds, "You're awful quiet, Claire."

"Yeah. Sorry. It's been a long day."

Destiny is forgiving of my flagging attention. She tells me she has had long days, too, so she understands.

Then she moves with her usual speed to another subject.

"You know what's weird? I kinda miss my studs. I mean, when I had those studs, I was like, you know, Bad Destiny."

"And you liked being bad?" I ask.

She considers her answer, then says, "Not bad like mean. Bad like . . . free." She smiles. "I used to wake up on Venice Beach, and there was the sun and the ocean, and I'd walk to the pier . . . and I was, like, free."

She means Santa Monica Pier, so I tell her about the girl.

"That sucks," Destiny says, though with little understanding that she might have exchanged places with this drowned girl, be in the morgue rather than with me. Instead her mind wheels back to Muriel.

"Last shift she reported me for having black fingernails," she says. "She told Cal that it was disgusting, made my fingers look dirty. He made me change. So now look."

She displays her hands, wiggles her fingers.

"What do you think?"

Her fingernails are purple.

6.

I'm back at home by nine.

I've left a few lights on, and as I pull into my driveway, I imagine that people are waiting for me inside. At first I see Max on the sofa, reading a history book but putting it down when I enter. After Max, it's Melody at the kitchen table, doing her homework, hoping it's correct, checking her arithmetic with Max and her English grammar with me.

My former life.

When I'd had a man to kiss at night and a daughter to hug before she left for school, someone to eat with and shop with, with whom I could confide and vent and share . . . everything.

Now when I think of people inside my house, my fear of Simon takes over, and I see a big man in a bulky jogging suit slapping a rubber truncheon as he comes toward me. I turn back toward the door, desperate to escape, but a second man is standing in front of it, blocking my way, a spool of black duct tape dangling like a bracelet from his thick wrist.

Even though I know these thugs are only imaginary, I look through my front window before going inside. If Mr. Cohen sees me doing this, it will alarm him, but I am compelled to do it anyway.

Once in the house, I methodically check the doors and windows.

Nothing is amiss. Everything is secure.

I walk down the corridor and into my bedroom.

In the adjoining bath, I remove my makeup, wash my face, brush my teeth, then undress and climb into my bed.

According to the evening news, there have been the usual number of accidents, traffic snarls, fires, city council resolutions. There is no mention of the girl.

I turn off the television and reach for my bedside book. It is about the dancing girls of Mumbai. Each night men go by the hundreds to the bars along Mira Road. Usually they simply wave folded wads of money at the girls, but sometimes they take garlands made of rupees and place them around the necks of their favorite performers. "The men think I dance for them," one of the girls says, "but it is the men who dance for me." There is no indication that this dancer is aware of the danger that resides in the weapon she wields, despite the fact that the bodies of bar dancers are regularly pulled from the excremental sludge of the Mithi River.

I read for half an hour, then close the book and turn out the light. Eventually I drift off to sleep, awaken, drift off again.

After a while I give up, go to my computer, and check my emails.

There's one from Mehdi. It's long, and somewhat rambling. He's talking about the wife who betrayed him.

He has often described her as a "seductress," though she hardly looks the part. He has to convince himself of her beauty, because if he does not have a beautiful wife, he is less of a man. Truth is truth, however, and in the pictures of her that he has shown me, she has sharp features and eyes that look almost hostilely at the camera, with a sour expression, as if she is irritated by its prying lens.

In present-day Iran, Mehdi writes, such a "harlot" would be stoned to death. He's quick to add that he is a "modern man" who doesn't approve of this: *Ha-ha . . . just saying.*

Just saying, yes.

And yet I sometimes imagine him in a crowd of men, hurling stones at the wife who betrayed him, her arms tied to her sides and her body buried waist-deep in the ground. Would he cheer ecstatically when a rock bloodied her face or cracked a bone?

Toward the end of his email, Mehdi switches his attention to me.

He has bought some Iranian pistachios and dates.

He will have these *for your pleasure* at our next class.

He wants to help me get more clients by designing a better flyer.

He wants to "succor" me.

Mehdi's suggestion is that I'm weak, in need of his guidance and instruction.

I find this insinuation both intrusive and insulting.

As a mental antidote, I switch on the television again. They're showing that old chestnut *Double Indemnity*. Barbara Stanwyck is pure seduction. Those dark glasses and loose-fitting clothes. The way she floats down the stairs. You can almost feel the hot breeze that wafts toward Fred MacMurray as she passes. Even without touching, they seem caught in a dark, erotic dance of lust and murder.

The phone rings.

I tell myself that there's nothing to fear. It's a client with a last-minute cancellation.

Or Ava, who seems hardly ever to sleep.

It isn't Simon, I assure myself as I answer it.

But it is.

"Don't hang up, Claire. I want to apologize. I overreacted."

Manipulation is all he knows. He'll try this, then that. Put on one mask. Exchange it for another. It's the kind of deception that has worked for him all his life.

"I'm sorry," he says. "That's why I'm calling. To tell you that I'm sorry about our last conversation. It ended on the wrong foot."

He means that it ended with him not being able to convince me to vanish from his life.

When I don't respond, he makes another effort.

"Can we meet? It's as much for you as it is for me."

This is a lie, and I know it. He wants to convince me that nothing I believe is true, or ever was.

I know what's coming, a spew of phony pity. I act to stop it.

"Is someone following me?" I blurt.

"Following you?"

He genuinely sounds surprised by the question. I know better.

"Have you hired someone to watch me, Simon?"

His surprise becomes amazement.

"What are you talking about, Claire? Why would I—?"

"Yes or no?"

"No!"

Now he'll feign being wounded by such a charge. He is once more the blameless object of a false accusation.

"My God, Claire, have you completely . . ."

He stops and abruptly changes his tone. Now he is all sweetness and concern.

"Claire, do you really believe that I would—"

"Do you think I'm hallucinating, Simon?"

He releases a long, weary breath.

"No one is following you, Claire," he tells me. "Okay? No one is following you."

There is a pause before he adds in a calm, reasoning tone, "But if you . . . think you're being followed, I could help with that."

"Help?" I snap. "You mean help me get rid of my paranoid visions?"

"I mean I could find you a . . . quiet place."

He is talking about a sanatorium of some kind. Rehab for my shattered mind. A nice little mountain retreat where I can regain my senses.

"And Claire, don't worry. I'll pay for it."

"Keep your money," I tell him fiercely. "I'm not crazy, Simon. I know what you did."

"Claire, please, I want you to—"

"I have nothing more to say to you."

"All right," Simon says like a man tired of arguing a case he can't win. "Then I'll let you go."

He sounds like an executioner apologizing for the ax. This is the real reason for his call. He can say to himself, *Okay, I gave you one last chance. You didn't take it. Whatever happens now, you brought it on yourself.*

"Goodbye, Claire."

Is it only my fear of him that makes this fare-well sound so final?

I put down my phone and walk into the living room.

I have hung a selection of reproductions. Mary Cassatt's *Mother and Child*. Marc Chagall's *Le Visage Bleu*. Tonight I am drawn to Van Gogh's portrait of his little room in Arles. There is anguish in every brushstroke, and yet he made something beautiful out of his life. If we could all do that, masterpieces would hang from every wall.

The blinking light of my answering machine tells me that I have a message. It's from my father, his voice dry and cracked with age.

"Hi, Claire. Any chance you might pick up some doughnuts on the way over tomorrow?"

Tomorrow.

Tuesday.

My once-a-week nod to his fatherhood.

I delete his message and head for my bedroom.

I keep two photographs of Melody on the table beside my bed.

In one of them, she is five years old, smiling, happy, cradled in her father's loving arms.

The second photograph is of Melody at four-teen. A scrim of trouble veils her features. She seems oddly distant and ill at ease, as if burdened with a dread she's afraid to share.

These two pictures rest side by side.

They divide my life into its twin phases.

Before and after Simon.

I pick up the more recent photograph of Melody. It was taken a year before that trip to Catalina.

Before the night I found her standing in the rain on the deck of the boat.

Before she told me about Simon.

Before I didn't believe her.

I peer at the picture silently but hear the promise I've made to myself:

I won't let him do it again.

PART II

SLOAN

WHEN I BECAME a sin eater, I looked up the derivation of the term. It turned out that a sin eater was a kind of magical figure who went to the house of a deceased human being and ate a ritual meal. The servings might be no more than a crust of bread along with some of the local beer to wash it down with. The important part was that this food and drink had absorbed the dead man's sins, and as it was eaten, all his evil deeds were absolved. He could go on to the afterlife completely free of his crimes.

The present-day Los Angeles version of a sin eater is also called a fixer or a cleaner. And of course sin eating isn't about food anymore. Most of the time it's about power, money, or the need to get even. Less often, it has to do with something more abstract, like getting back your self-respect. More rarely, it's a question of regaining trust after someone you'd deeply believed in proved to be other than what you thought he was.

After I left the LAPD, sin eating seemed a natural fit for me. I'd learned how to investigate crimes, how the courts work, how lawyers talk, how pleas are bargained. I knew how to mollify volatile people, negotiate without anger, deal with individuals who had inflated ideas of their own importance. I was cool under pressure, persuasive even to people who were initially disinclined to be reasonable. I was tough when I needed to be but always eager to compromise. Just as important, sin eating was a business that didn't require a license or any further training, academic or otherwise. It was ready to hand. All I had to do was hang a sign.

As far as I can see, there's only one thing about the profession of sin eating that hasn't changed since it began: a sin eater doesn't require much space.

Or much furniture, either. In my office on Venice Boulevard, there is a desk, a computer, a filing cabinet, and a closet where I store the tools of my trade. Articles of disguise: mostly wigs and an assortment of eyeglasses. Stationery with phony letterheads. Recording devices. Surveillance cameras and GPS tracking equipment. A safe that usually contains a few thousand dollars in cash, along with a fully licensed 9mm automatic.

The job is as uncomplicated as the tools it requires. Simply put, I clean up the messes made by people who have big names and a lot of money. I make sure they don't suffer the consequences of the reckless things they do. I calm down irate wives or lovers. I work to keep my clients' names off the police blotter or a courtroom docket. That way I ensure that the painful results of bad behavior are either modified or disappear entirely. It's usually a matter of cash, the only question being how much. Sin eaters bring down the price, convince the troublesome party that their client is not a money tree whose greenback leaves can endlessly be plucked. In that sense, I'm a broker between two extremes. Fifty percent of my time, I try to get one side to be reasonable. The other fifty percent I spend doing the same for the opposite party.

"Good morning," Jake said when I stepped out of the elevator.

Jake is a retired LAPD homicide detective who now works as a private investigator. He rents the office next to mine, rarely closes his door, and so is always aware of when I come and go. He's a friendly, talkative man, but since my father's death, I've lost the gift for idle conversation.

As for Jake, he's tall without being gangly and says he once had movie-star looks. He means this as a joke, but I can see that he was probably quite good-looking in his younger days. His face reminds me of Charles, the one long relationship I've had.

I caught Charles's eye at a New Year's Eve party at the law firm where he worked. He couldn't believe a cop could be so "fly." Three months later I moved into his apartment in Westwood. For a long time we were happy. We thought about getting married, having kids. But my being a cop made trouble for us. He couldn't handle how tense and driven the job made me. He wanted me to quit, but I kept at it, always with the idea of becoming commissioner one day. He said I was only trying to achieve that high office because my father had failed to reach it. He was probably right. That didn't matter. We argued. Everything went south. I moved out.

Being without him made things worse.

The job wore me down.

Two years later I left the LAPD and switched to sin eating.

For the first year it was hard going. I was an unknown commodity, new to the business. There weren't many clients. Over time more showed up at my door. Within three years I'd gotten a reputation for handling problems in a "nice" way, using more brains than brawn. If you needed a bone-breaker, you'd go to someone else. But if you wanted a sin eater who would carefully scope out the situation, then get it solved with as little messiness as possible, the word was, *Get Sloan Wilson.*

The one thing I hadn't expected when I began this new work was how much I'd later come to like it. There was good to be done in this profession. There was a place for calm understanding and wise restraint. I didn't have to be a bully or threaten people with bodily harm. I didn't have to shout in their faces. I could simply listen to their tales of woe. How they'd been used, betrayed, cheated, misled. After that I could figure out what they really wanted in the wake of this mistreatment and go from there.

What I brought to sin eating, as a client once said to me, was "the female touch."

By the time I was five years into the job, I no longer thought of returning to the LAPD. I had found my calling. It was good. I was close—really close—to being happy.

My father noticed how much I'd changed and never talked about my leaving the force. "You're going to be okay," he told me not long before he died.

I thought he was right, and was pleased that as he'd approached his end, he'd felt that my life was on a steady course.

In fact, the only unfortunate thing I saw in my future was that I wouldn't be able to share its little victories with my father anymore. This was the thought that was still lingering in my mind when I got to my office that morning.

"Get a good night's sleep?" Jake asked cheerfully as I swept by his open door.

"Sure," I said.

Which wasn't true.

"Only sweet dreams, right?" Jake added with a broad wink.

"Always." Also not true.

In fact, I'd once again woken at daybreak,

already tired from having gotten no sleep, my morning mood battered by a very bad dream. The same one I'd had off and on since my father died.

I'm in a city that's falling apart. There are rioters everywhere, smashing windows, overturning cars, setting buildings on fire. To make it worse, a hard rain is falling, cold and oily, slithering down windows, leaving a black stain. I somehow have to get my father through all this. He is dying, but somewhere in this maze of buildings there is a machine that can save him.

I keep trying to find it. But I never do.

I'd still been drifting in the aftermath of that nightmare when I reached my office. To pull myself out of it, I got right down to my clients' troubles. A midlevel Hollywood actor with a paternity problem. A movie director with an unflattering tabloid story he wanted me to squelch. A business executive whose blackmailer I must convince to find another means of livelihood.

I was still working on these affairs when Jake popped his head into my office and said I should break for lunch. I wasn't hungry, but he didn't like to eat alone.

At the diner Jake talked about his family, his grandchildren, a joke his wife had told him. While he talked, I watched kids playing in the schoolyard across the street. They looked happy and full of energy.

"You keeping radio silence?" Jake asked.

I faked a smile, as if I were returning to the old, less somber version of myself.

"No, just thinking," I answered.

Jake didn't press the issue. He switched the conversation to a case he was working on. Viola Walker had been found dead in her garage in Brentwood. She'd been shot execution style, in the back of the head. No sign of sexual assault. According to the crime-scene inventory, she'd had a Hermès Bleu alligator bag that clocked in at a whopping $68,000. The wallet tucked inside was gray leather, Gucci. It bulged with $4,000 in bills of different sizes, but mostly hundreds. Clearly robbery had not been the motive. It was the husband who'd hired Jake to look into his wife's murder, as well as to keep tabs on the official investigation, which Jake could easily do through his contacts in the department.

"I figure it's probably meant to send a message to the husband," Jake said. "Maybe he stiffed someone he shouldn't have."

"Then why not kill the husband?"

"Because the killer wants the money, and the wife isn't good for that. She probably didn't know a thing about any of it." He took a sip of coffee. "Death must have come as a complete surprise to her."

To die that fast struck me as a very good thing. My father's death had taken eight months.

There'd been times, when he slept and I'd known he'd awaken only to pain, when a bullet to the head had seemed the right thing to do.

"Anyway, the husband is convinced the cops have pegged him for the murder. I'm supposed to find a better suspect."

I glanced out toward a building that had once been a movie theater but was now a bank. My mother had taken me to a movie there. She'd been in her midthirties then, and very beautiful. People turned to watch her pass. When they did, she enjoyed it. But that day she'd been nervous, always glancing around, checking her watch. I'd known something was up. I might even have asked her what the problem was if he hadn't shown up before I got the chance.

She pretended he was a friend.

He wore a white suit and a large white hat, both of which gave him a theatrical air. I heard her call him Harry. Just Harry. She never said his last name.

They'd chatted for a while. Very discreetly. No holding hands, and certainly no kissing. And yet I'd sensed an intimacy between them, as if they were sharing secrets. I'd been too young to make out a lover when I saw one, but in later years I'd come to realize that that is what this Harry must have been to my mother.

Even a few minutes after lunch, when I was in my office, I kept thinking about the shadowy bedroom with my father's body. I knew I had to shake myself out this mood and get back to normal, but my recent grief and heartbreak still had their teeth sunk very deeply into me, and they were holding on. Each time I tried to raise my spirits—laugh at a joke or make one of my own—I felt them drag me down.

It's dangerous to feel that in some part of your life, the rug's been pulled out from under you. I didn't want to feel that way, but I did.

I knew it was temporary, however. Like everything else, I'd get over losing my father, and life would seem good to me again. Soon, I told myself, everything will get back its shine.

2.

I was at my desk later that afternoon when Maurice Walker arrived. He was dressed in a blue pinstripe suit. He was of medium height, with gray hair. He'd brought with him another man who looked to be in his midforties, trim and athletic, the type who regularly hits the gym. They went directly into Jake's office.

I knew the routine. Jake would ask the usual questions. He'd want to know who might have had a motive to kill Walker's wife. Revenge would be explored. A disgruntled associate? A business deal gone bad? Could drugs have been involved? Did Mrs. Walker have a life insurance policy? From there, Jake would ask about the state of their marital relations. Whether things were fine between Walker and his wife, and if not, did either have a lover?

They emerged from Jake's office just over an hour later. I was standing by the water cooler as all three of them made their way to the elevator.

Just to be polite, Jake introduced me, though almost comically. "Sloan here is a sin eater," he said.

Walker just nodded, but the other man looked at me curiously.

76

"What's a sin eater?" he asked.

Because I'd dealt with that question before, I had a ready answer for it, one I'd adapted to Los Angeles by using a Movietown reference.

"Did you ever see *Pulp Fiction*?" I asked.

"Of course. It's one of my favorites. I've seen it three or four times."

"Then you'll remember a scene where two bunglers kill a man in the back of a car," I said. "They have to have the whole thing cleaned up. To get it done, they call a guy who specializes in, well, making things go away."

The man smiled knowingly. "Ah, yes. He comes and fixes the situation. Wipes up the blood. The fingerprints. Everything."

"In a way, that's what I do," I said. "Only without the blood, and I don't get involved with murders."

I offered my friendly sin-eater smile.

"I'm more of a gentle persuader," I added.

"And if that doesn't work?" the man asked.

On cue, my smile vanished and I showed him my hard side. "At that point I'd go to Plan B."

He seemed to appreciate my profession, and looked at me almost admiringly.

"A woman who makes bad things go away," he said with a smile. "Very interesting."

He thrust out his hand.

"Simon Miller," he told me. "Pleased to meet you."

I shook his hand.

The elevator opened.

Miller started to get into it but stopped and turned to face me.

"Was your father Monroe Wilson?" he asked.

"Yes, he was. How did you know?"

"As I passed your office, I noticed his picture on the table behind your desk." He smiled. "My father sat on the county commission. He often spoke of your father. About what a good cop he was. He thought he had a great career ahead of him. Then your father suddenly retired, right?"

"Yes, he did."

"So how's he doing, your dad?"

"He died. A month ago."

I recalled the day of his burial, how few people had attended the graveside ceremony. Mostly old men from the LAPD, at rest with their plaques and their pensions. After the final prayer they'd trailed down to their waiting cars, leaving me alone with my love for him.

"I'm very sorry," Miller said. "My dad died three years ago. It's a tough moment."

"Yes, it is."

"I really am very sorry," he repeated.

I could see that something was threading through his mind. He didn't tell me what it was, and I didn't ask.

"Well, goodbye," he said.

"Goodbye."

I thought that would be the end of it, but he called an hour later.

"I need a sin eater," he said. "Not that I have any sins to eat. But I do have a problem."

"What kind of problem?"

"I'd rather show you." He gave me his address, said it was urgent. He wanted to know if I could come to his house right away.

I told him I'd drop by later in the afternoon.

Which I did.

He lived in a large house in Beverly Hills. Spanish style, with a red tile roof. There was a BMW in the driveway as well as a Bentley.

I had to wait at the door only a couple of seconds after ringing the bell.

"Welcome," he said.

He'd shed the jacket and tie and was now dressed in a white shirt and black trousers.

"I've done a little research on you," he said as he escorted me into a room just off the foyer. "You were with the LAPD for ten years. Made it up to Homicide Division in record time. Youngest ever. Then you left the department. Why?"

There'd been many reasons. I'd never been particularly good at department politics. The higher I rose, the more I had to watch my back. I saw too much neglect of duty, too much waste of money, too much indulgence of incompetence, especially as a result of cronyism. In addition, the paperwork grew each year, as did the time required to sit at a desk and fill out the necessary forms. I liked being on the street. Unfortunately, I was as office-bound as a bank clerk.

But it wasn't just a question of problems in the department itself.

The whole system was disillusioning. Good cases were blown by lazy prosecutions. Judges threw out vital evidence. The revolving door kept revolving, and with each turn more bad people were set free to do bad things. As for dispensing justice, that mostly happened in the movies.

In the end I'd talked it all over with my father. His only comment had been a rather melancholy, "Then it's time to leave. Because if you stay, you'll end up a bad cop."

It was this response that had finally sent me running for the exit. The fear that if I remained in the LAPD, I would fail to be the kind of cop my father had been.

I didn't want to discuss any of this with Miller, however, so I plucked another reason from the list.

"I guess I just got tired of never being able to stop a murder before it happened," I answered. "In homicide, you're always one step behind a killer. And when the victim is a woman or a child, it can feel sort of . . . useless."

"But when you catch a killer, that brings a little closure, doesn't it?"

"It does for some people. It didn't for me."

Miller smiled. "Interesting."

We talked a few minutes longer before Miller got down to business.

"I have a problem with my ex-wife. She has a history of mental instability. Rather than go into the details, I'd like to show you something."

With that, he directed me down a long corridor.

"This is an old movie-era house," he said. "It has a screening room."

There were statues and paintings of little angels playing on harps. Even the small ones were in huge wooden frames with elaborate carvings.

At the end of the hall he guided me into a curtained room. There were two rows of movie seats. Red. Cushioned.

"Have a seat."

I did.

A large flat-screen television was mounted to the wall. The usual audiovisual equipment rested in a cabinet just below it. Miller placed a DVD in the player, picked up the remote control, and took the seat next to me.

"I had a technician put this together," Miller said. "He knows all about audiovisual equipment. You can tell it's spliced, of course. We had to do that because it's shot from three different angles. One camera is trained on the front driveway. The other is on the house. The third one is from high above. It takes in both the driveway and the house."

"You have a lot of security cameras."

"When you see this, you'll know why I had them installed."

He looked at me sadly.

"Honestly, since this happened, I feel like I've been living under siege."

He tapped a button on the remote, and the black screen flickered to life.

I watched as a white PT Cruiser circled the driveway, then came to a halt in front of Simon's house. A blond woman is sitting behind the wheel. She bows her head. She looks like she's hesitating, or perhaps doesn't quite know what to do next. It's as if she's standing on a bridge, staring down at the water, deciding if she really has to jump. She remains this way for about fifteen seconds. During that time she hardly moves. You can feel things churning inside her. She is considering the consequences one last time. I'd seen that expression before. A kid with a gun, figuring out if he truly wants to shoot a cop, take it that far, change his life that much for the worse.

The kid usually puts down the gun.

The woman made a different choice.

She gets out of the car. Her hair is long and straight, and she is very thin. She moves slowly. There is a sense of physical weakness, of her being in bad health. A woman who isn't eating enough or getting enough sleep. When she raises the rear door of the Cruiser, it almost seems too heavy for her. She uses both arms to raise it. Then she stops again. Her arms dangle at her sides. Given all that, it's hard for me to imagine that she doesn't just close the door, pull herself back behind the wheel, and drive away. It would be so much easier to do that.

But that's not what she does.

She takes out a can of paint, opens it, and walks over to a dark blue Lexus. With a broad brush, she scrawls the words CHILD MOLESTER across the entire driver's side of the car in blood-red paint.

I looked over at Miller. He was staring expressionlessly at the screen. I couldn't tell whether he was hiding his feelings for this woman or simply didn't have any left to offer her. He was calm, steady. It was as if he'd gotten used to her being crazy, to being attacked by her.

I turned back to the screen.

The woman has finished her work on the Lexus. She steps back and looks at the words she's written. Then she moves to the front door of the house and angrily, sloppily writes the same words: CHILD MOLESTER.

The video moves to another camera. A police cruiser pulls into the driveway and two uniformed officers get out. The woman turns to face them. She stands and waits as the two officers approach. One of them puts her hand on her pistol. I recognize her as Candace Marks. We'd been rookies together, but she'd later gone on to get a degree in criminal justice and now worked in the Internal Affairs Department, reaching for a pencil instead of a gun.

Candace does all the talking. Her male partner just watches as she steps toward the woman, raises her hand, then brings it down in a slow, fluid motion. She is instructing the woman to put down the paint and the brush.

The woman doesn't do it.

Candace stops going toward her.

They stare at each other.

Finally the woman speaks. There is no way of knowing what she says, but I can see that it puts Candace on alert. Her eyes get more intense. She glances at her partner. I have seen that signal. It means, *We've got real trouble here.*

"This is the hard part to watch," Simon said. "It hurts me to see it."

I don't look at him. Part of me is no longer even in his house, sitting in a dark room, watching a television screen.

I am outside now.

With the woman.

She watches the two police officers as they approach. Candace is in the lead, a few paces in front of the second officer. She is trying to talk her down. Motioning for her to let go of the paint can, the brush. The woman holds on to them. She is very still.

The second officer steps to the right. The woman's head jerks toward him. She sees the maneuver for what it is, an effort to surround her. She flings the can toward Candace. A wave of red paint sloshes out of the can as it hurtles through the air.

Technically, this is assault.

I know what will happen next.

The police rush forward and bring her first to her knees, then facedown on the stone driveway. She resists, kicks, struggles. Candace straddles her, brings her right and left wrists together, and cuffs her.

Miller comes out. He looks relieved that the incident is over. The police lift her from the ground and lead her to their car. Candace places her hand on top of the woman's head as she lowers her into the back seat.

Miller shakes hands with Candace and her partner. He is obviously thanking them.

Once they've gone, he turns and goes inside.

At this point the screen goes black.

"That was five years ago," Miller said.

He got to his feet, walked over to the TV.

"The woman is my ex-wife," he told me. "Her name is Claire Fontaine."

"Where'd she get that idea about you?" I asked him. "That you're a child molester?"

"It had to do with her daughter from a previous marriage. Melody. She drowned one night near

85

Catalina. Later Claire became convinced that I'd molested her."

I had no way of judging any of this, but that wasn't important. You give your clients the benefit of the doubt and do all you can to help them.

Even so, I pursued the issue for one additional step.

"This idea about you came out of the blue?" I asked.

"Out of the blue."

"No one else has ever accused you of this?"

Miller looked offended. "Absolutely not. And by the way, I'm not the only man she's accused of terrible things. Her own father, as a matter of fact. According to Claire, when she was eight years old, her father tried to drown her."

"Why?" I asked.

"He fell in love with a woman who didn't want any kids around. So he took Claire swimming and at some point tried to drown her. Claire says he grabbed her ankles when she was trying to climb out of the water onto a boat, tried to pull her underwater. He would have succeeded if some other people hadn't shown up. After that her father lost the woman, and for that reason he never stopped hating Claire."

He released an exasperated sigh.

"She never had any evidence of that story, either," he added.

He shook his head.

"But once Claire has something in her mind, evidence doesn't matter. It's the same with me and her child-molestation accusation."

"But that was five years ago," I reminded him. "What's the problem with her now?"

"She's having another breakdown."

He took out the DVD and replaced it with another.

"What you're about to see now is from four days ago. This was taken by surveillance cameras from my fiancée's daughter's school. The headmaster of the school is an old friend of mine and so he made a copy for me."

He hit the Play button and the screen came to life.

The video shows the same white PT Cruiser parked across from the Larsen School. Claire sits behind the wheel, staring intently toward the building's front gate. She does not get out. She barely moves. She looks like a sniper. A clock records the passing time.

"She sat there for three hours," Miller said when the screen went black again. "Three hours, just watching."

"Did the school call the police?"

"No," Miller answered. "There's really no law against someone sitting in a car. And they didn't know Claire. They didn't perceive any danger."

He returned to the seat beside me.

"I wouldn't have known about this if Charlotte hadn't spotted Claire when she went to pick up her daughter."

"Charlotte?"

"My fiancée. I'm getting married soon. That's probably what set Claire off. Charlotte has a daughter named Emma. She is about the same age as Melody was when I married Claire. Claire thinks that I am going to 'do it again.' That's the phrase she used when she wrote to me. 'I'm not going to let you do it again.' "

He said that he'd later called her. He'd wanted to deal with Claire personally rather than take this issue to the authorities.

"I don't want her to be arrested again," he said. "I'm trying to protect her . . . from herself. I'm floundering, I admit it. Which is why I called you. I don't know what to do in this situation."

He knew there were steps that he could have taken, given her stalking behavior at the school. But he'd tried to reason with Claire first. Unfortunately, she'd not been willing to discuss the issue with him.

"She practically hung up on me," Miller said. "But not before accusing me of having her followed. Which is completely ridiculous."

"Why does she think she's being followed?" I asked.

Miller shrugged. "How do I know? Maybe

she saw something she took to be suspicious. Or maybe she didn't see anything at all."

He released a tortured breath.

"I'm getting married in three weeks. My concern is that whatever Claire intends to do, she will do it before then. Because she wants to stop the marriage."

"That's not much time."

I could see real fear in his eyes. "She has a gun," he told me.

"What kind of gun?"

"A pistol. She showed it to me. It's an old relic that belonged to her first husband, but as far as I know, it still works."

He looked at me in a way that told me I should take this gun quite seriously.

"Look, you may think I'm in a panic," he said, "but when I think about last time, the nutty thing she did, and how angry she is now, I have to consider just how far she might go this time."

His tone became imploring, the voice of a man who really needed help.

"I know I could hire bodyguards. But I don't want to live like a prisoner. I don't want Charlotte or Emma to live that way, either."

"Do you think she might harm them, too?" I asked.

"I can't say what she might do. That's the problem. She's crazy."

He looked like a little boy who needed

assurance that everything was going to be all right.

I knew that the moment of truth had arrived. "What exactly do you want me to do?" I asked.

Miller hesitated, a common response to this question. People who hire sin eaters are often reluctant to get to the point of no return.

Miller, like others I've known, took a round-about way of getting there.

"Earlier you told me that you left the LAPD because you could never stop a murder before it happened," he said finally. "Maybe this time you can."

He seemed alarmed by his own dark thoughts. "I'm afraid of her, Sloan. I'm afraid of what she might do."

I considered the possibility that Miller was exaggerating the danger posed by his ex-wife. Sure, the video showed a distraught woman, but sloshing paint onto a car, or even hurling a paint can at a cop, was a far cry from killing someone. That didn't really matter, however, because by then I'd learned that it is as easy to underestimate a person's potential for violence as it is to overestimate it. Miller was asking me to protect him, his fiancée, and her daughter from a woman whose behavior in both the past and the present scared him. She was a threat he wanted me to contain or neutralize. I'd had quite a few other clients in more or less the same situation, and I'd always been able to provide the service that was required. I saw no reason to feel that this particular case was any different from those previous ones.

And so I took the job.

"I'll need Claire's address and phone number," I said.

He gave them to me.

"Where does she work?" I asked.

"No particular place. She's a French teacher. Freelance. She goes from client to client."

"Does she still drive the same car?"

"Yes."

"Is it the only one she has?"

"As far as I know."

"Does Charlotte live with you?"

"No."

"I'll need her address."

"Why?"

"So I'll know if Claire gets near her house."

Miller looked at me quizzically.

"I can keep track of her electronically," I told him. "No one needs to follow anyone anymore. Not physically, at least. If I see that she's headed toward any of you, I'll let you know."

"Good. I'd appreciate that."

"In the meantime, I'll work on other ways to . . ." I paused because the word struck me as inordinately brutal. "Contain her."

Miller suddenly looked relieved. He offered his hand. I took it with a firm grip.

"Thank you," Miller said.

That's how it began.

The end of my career.

3.

At the end of the day, Jake asked if I wanted to play a game of pool after work. I turned him down. Instead I went home.

The house was small and cozy, but when I went into it that evening, I felt the familiar chill of my father's absence. I'd moved back in during his illness, done all I could to care for him. He'd put up a brave front, tried to make the best of it, even to the point of concealing his pain.

None of that was on my mind, however.

In fact, as I made dinner I hardly thought of my father's recent death. It was his life that concerned me, particularly the way my mother had ruined his career in the LAPD by lodging a false accusation of corruption.

She'd made her charge in what the commissioner had later described to my father as a "crazy phone call." She'd offered no details and provided no evidence for her accusation. My father was dirty, according to her, though not in the usual way. She never said that he took bribes. Money wasn't the issue. What he wanted was to be commissioner. He did favors in order to get favors in return. A good word at the right moment that would bump him up the chain of command. He was, she said, "ambition's whore."

A week after that phone call, she'd gone into the little office my father had at home, taken the revolver from his desk, and shot herself in the head.

I'd come home from school later than usual that day. Like always, I'd expected to find the back door open. But it was locked. So I'd walked around to the front. Once inside the house, I'd called for my mother, but there'd been no answer. I'd gone from room to room until I'd found her in my father's office.

She was lying on the floor with her legs drawn up under her. I could see only one side of her face, along with the blood that had pooled around it. For a few seconds I'd just stood there, too shocked to move or even cry for help. In that silence, it felt like everything had died.

I'd been only seven years old at the time. I'd known nothing about how completely she'd ruined my father. But over the years he had revealed the story bit by bit. By the time I entered the police academy, I'd put it all together.

Along with her accusation, my mother's subsequent suicide had sealed the case against him. Her charge didn't have to be true. And she might have had a hundred different reasons for killing herself. But put the two together, and who would appoint a police commissioner whose wife had killed herself after making such a phone call?

It was these grim events that explained my father's abrupt retirement, followed by his sadness and disappointment, the isolated life he'd lived after that, with none of his old comrades by his side.

After my mother died, he'd struggled to raise me, supporting a single-parent household by working several jobs at once. He was a security guard at a department store, parked cars at the Ivy, manned the entrance gate at various movie studios. It was by doing such work that he'd paid the fees for my parochial school, bought me nice shoes and dresses so I wouldn't look poor, and even managed to scrape up the money for my senior trip to New York City when I was seventeen.

Thinking of all this stoked the resentment I'd always felt against my mother's cruel allegations, but it also reminded me of Simon Miller, of what his ex-wife was once again attempting to do to him. Like my father's, his life was being ruined by a woman's accusations.

After a quick dinner, I went through the material Miller had given me a few hours before.

Claire's official records were gathered together in a single incident report that was long and thorough. A psychiatric evaluation was included, along with a "profile" that provided a general view of what she'd done in the wake of Melody's death, which was to divorce Miller almost immediately.

But it didn't stop there.

During the following weeks, she'd written letters to Miller's law firm as well as to the California bar.

Miller didn't take this lying down. He got a restraining order against her. Things got worse and worse. Finally Claire went to Simon's house with a can of red paint. She wrote CHILD MOLESTER on his door and on his car. He called the cops. When they showed up, she fought. It was pretty clear that she was out of it, so the court ordered an evaluation by a state psychiatrist named Dr. Frederick Lind. According to Dr. Lind's report, Claire claimed her father had tried to kill her. Lind thought this accusation was connected to the one against Miller. She'd offered no evidence for either case.

There were other findings.

Claire Fontaine was

Suspicious and mistrustful of others.
Convinced that others lied about her.
Convinced that she was being persecuted.
Socially isolated.
Aggressive and hostile.

This had been followed by a stark diagnosis: *paranoia.*

Claire had stayed in a mental hospital for three months and been released only on condition that she would leave Simon Miller alone.

Miller had tucked two photographs into the same envelope. One was of Charlotte, an elegant woman in her early forties. Her clothes were expensive, though not ostentatious. She obviously had money, or came from it, but she wore her wealth easily, comfortably, like an old ring. The picture of Emma showed a girl in a loose-fitting summer dress. She is standing on the beach, her back to the sea, waving toward the camera. Her hair is long and blond, and her eyes are a shining blue. She looks happy, carefree, a radiant little girl.

My father believed that a homicide cop should always keep the victim's actual self in mind. You had to look at a murdered person and say to yourself that this was a real person, with all sorts of feelings. A man, woman, or child who'd deserved to live and should have been given that chance.

I decided to take my father's advice, do the same with Charlotte and Emma but with a different mission. My job was to prevent their being harmed rather find who'd harmed them.

After reading through Claire's file, I decided that she could, in fact, be dangerous.

For that reason, I dug a little deeper into her, though not so much her past as her present. I wanted to know what she was up to when she was writing threatening letters to Simon Miller.

I started with her job and Googled "French Instruction. Claire Fontaine." Her website popped up, complete with a photograph of Claire dressed very professionally and smiling warmly. You'd have thought she was completely normal emotionally and entirely professional in terms of her career. She expressed herself well and presented herself as the soul of reason. She'd devised a ten-question test by which her prospective clients could determine their current level.

Her web page mirrored her perfectly practical presentation of herself. There were no videos. No music or fancy graphics. Everything was completely by the board.

I looked at her ads on Thumbtack, Yelp, and Craigslist and found the same bare-bones approach.

Next I did a broader search and found her name scattered about here and there. A certain Loraine Ferguson had posted a photograph of her high school class, and there was Claire in her cap and gown, her face barely visible in a crowd of other students.

In a brief obituary, she was mentioned as the widow of Max Slater, thirty-seven, a civil engineer who'd died of cancer.

There were other mentions of her, but they didn't add much in terms of her character, interests, or anything else. At twenty-three, for example, she'd been in the cast of a Venice, California, takeoff production of *The Merchant of Venice*. Claire had played a flower seller. Max Slater had been cast as "a villainous debt collector," so this may have been how they met.

Public records revealed their later marriage, the birth of their daughter, Melody, and their purchase of a house in Mid-Wilshire, all perfectly ordinary citations.

Five years after her husband's death, she'd married Simon Miller. Since Miller was so prominent, there'd been a short piece about the wedding in the *LA Times*, complete with a photograph of the happy couple, Claire in a white lacy gown, holding a bouquet, Miller in coat and tails.

After that, Claire's life went dark.

On May 7, 2013, Melody's body was found on a Catalina beach. According to the local news coverage, she'd been the victim of an accident. A later autopsy had indicated drowning as the cause of her death, with no suspicion of foul play.

Claire didn't appear in the news again until June 4 of that same year. She'd evidently left Miller almost immediately following Melody's death. But a month later she'd showed up at his house with a can of paint. The story took up a single column, and from experience I could see that it had been compiled from whatever police report had been filed on the incident.

For the next five years Claire's name did not appear in any public documents.

But she was back now, threatening Simon Miller, as well as his fiancée, Charlotte, and her daughter, Emma.

I had to protect them.

In order to do that, I'd need to keep track of Claire 24/7.

Later that night I drove to the address Miller had given me. Claire's car was parked on the street about a block from her house. I pulled over to the curb nearby, took a magnetized GPS tracker from my glove compartment, and walked back to the white PT Cruiser I'd seen in the video. The street was pretty much deserted. I didn't have to linger before attaching it to the bottom of the chassis.

When I got back to my house, I drew up a containment strategy for Claire. When I'd finished assembling the elements of my plan, I calculated the time involved and estimated my fee. As always, I allowed for various contingencies that might increase the price. Once this was done, I filled in the blanks of my usual boilerplate contract and emailed it to Miller for his approval.

Nothing in this process was other than routine.

But life has a way of unexpectedly turning one thing into another: a high school crush into a marriage, a first job into a way of life, a simple plan into a tragedy.

It was past midnight by then, so I was a bit surprised that Miller got back to me within minutes, agreed to my fee, then added a final note: *Whatever you have to do.*

I filed this email in a computer folder just like the rest of them. I labeled it *Claire Fontaine* and assumed that her case would be no different from others I'd worked on. I would solve Simon Miller's problem. It would all be neat and clean, and when it was over, I'd collect my fee and move on.

At that point my attention should have easily shifted to another client. Instead I continued to think about Claire, what she'd done to Miller, what she was threatening to do to him again, a train of thought that brought my mother storming back into my mind. As the minutes passed, these two women merged in a sinister and insidious way, my hatred for my mother bleeding into my feelings for Claire Fontaine.

Bleeding, I would think later. Yes. That was the right word.

CLAIRE

RAY PATRICK IS sitting by the window at the Starbucks when I arrive. He's dressed in white trousers and a light blue shirt, dark blue suede loafers with a tassel, no socks. These clothes come from some high-end store on Rodeo Drive. He is tall, slender, with salt-and-pepper hair.

He rises as I come toward him and offers his hand when I reach him. "Nice to meet you, Claire."

He holds my hand for just a single extended beat. "Would you like coffee?" he asks.

I shake my head, then notice the book he was reading as I came in. A biography of Leonardo da Vinci he's placed on the table.

I nod toward the photo of Leonardo on the cover.

"His first memory was of a bird. After that, he was obsessed with flight."

Ray seems pleased by this little story. "You know a lot about him, I see."

"He was sort of my specialty in college."

"Ava mentioned that you studied art in Paris."

"The history of art. I'm not a painter."

"I'm not either. I just sell what others paint."

This strikes me as gently self-deprecating, a trait I like in people.

In that way, Ray reminds me of Max. There is the same ready smile. I tell myself that such comparisons are fruitless, as well as unfair to Ray, or any other man I might meet.

Ray leans back slightly.

"When did you begin to study French?"

No one has asked me that question in a long time. Perhaps that's why it powerfully returns me to that earlier life. As if I have it in my hand, I see my widowed grandmother's letter asking me to come to Paris, opening her house to me, offering to provide for my education. I see her elegant French handwriting: *Tu seras en sécurité ici.* You will be safe here.

Loin de ton père. Far from your father.

She alone had believed me.

She'd even tried to persuade my father to let me go to France as a way of protecting me. He'd refused. *Why would I let a woman who thinks I'm a monster raise my daughter?*

Such had been his only explanation.

When I was eighteen, it had no longer been up to him, however, and so I'd accepted my grandmother's offer and taken the first plane to Paris.

"I got the opportunity to live in France," I tell Ray. "In Paris."

"How long were you there?"

"Four years. While I went to college."

"Were those the best years of your life?"

"Among them, yes."

"You knew a little French before going there, I suppose."

"Why do you suppose that?"

"Your name—Fontaine."

"That was my father's name, but he didn't speak French. It was my mother who was French. She taught me from the time I was a baby. She started with her favorite word."

"Which was?"

"Amour."

I expect to begin the lesson immediately, but his tone remains casually conversational. "Are most of your clients adults?" he asks.

"About half."

"How old is the youngest?"

"Four."

"That must be a challenge."

"Not really. I like teaching children. They can be so . . . absorbent."

"Can be, but not always, right?"

"Not always."

"This four-year-old, is it a girl or a boy?"

"A little girl."

"They can be quite charming, little girls."

"Little boys can be charming, too," I tell him.

He nods. "Of course."

I take out my notebook. "Shall we begin?"

I don't know why, but during the lesson every word in the vocabulary I teach Ray calls up a swirling tide of memory.

Maison. House.

During the interval between my saying a word and Ray repeating it, the world seems to stop, and time ebbs and flows on a series of images.

The house I lived in with my mother. The smell of bread. *La bûche de Noël* she baked for the season.

That same house without her, my room locked against any intrusion from my father, those sleepless nights when I feared he might try again, press a pillow over my face and lean all his weight into it.

My grandmother's high-windowed apartment on Boulevard Raspail; looking down from its balcony.

The house I shared with Max and Melody, its backyard strewn with toys, palm leaves floating in a plastic swimming pool.

The house I return to each night.

Dark.

Silent.

Empty.

"*May-sohn,*" Ray says.

"No," I correct him. "*May-zohn.* The *s* here is pronounced *z.*"

"In French the *s* is pronounced like a *z?*" Ray asks.

"When it comes between two vowels, yes," I tell him before going on to the next word.

"*Voiture,*" I say. "Car."

Now I am a little girl in the back seat of our family car, the windows rolled down, the desert sweeping out in all directions, the rounded boulders of Joshua Tree rising before us, my mother suddenly excited: *Look, Claire. A coyote.*

Then she is gone, and I am in the passenger seat of that same heavy black car, eating an ice cream and trying to be happy but mindful of the oddly stricken look on my father's face as he accelerates suddenly, only to slow down just as suddenly, as if caught in the grip of a fearful indecision. *Where are we going, Dad?* How grimly he'd given his answer: *For a swim.*

Ray sees none of this. We go through the words I choose in order to illustrate French pronunciations. He catches on a little faster than usual for someone who has never studied a foreign language. It's his mental stamina I notice. While many people are exhausted at the end of a lesson, Ray is clearly energized.

The lesson runs over an hour, but thanks to Ray's enthusiasm it seems much shorter.

He tries to pay me for the additional time. "It's only fair," he says as he offers me the money.

"No, thank you."

Devotion, commitment, passion. There should be no extra charge for these values. I take his $50 and we agree to meet at the same time in two days.

"I hope you had as much fun as I did," Ray tells me.

"Yes, I did."

"You have a lot of patience, Claire," he says when I turn to leave.

I look back at him. "Thank you."

On the way out, I see a group of teenaged girls heading across the parking lot. They are carrying their school bags. Talking and laughing.

After that, it's Ray Patrick who captures my attention. I watch as he walks to his car, a black Mercedes. There is an elegance to his stride, the sort one sees in men who are completely comfortable in their own skins.

I realize that I like him, and this attitude seems warm and natural and safe, a feeling I enjoy during the brief interval before I coldly remind myself that I'd liked Simon, too.

A call comes in while I'm driving to my next client. It's from Linda Bergman, who runs a service that provides translators "for all occasions."

A French tourist has been taken to Cedars-Sinai.

"Her name is Delphine Perron," Linda says. "She's evidently traveling on her own, so there's nobody here to help her. She fainted right on Hollywood Boulevard. The hospital wants to make sure she understands what the doctors tell her. Room 517 at two o'clock. Can you make it?"

I glance at my watch. I will have only thirty minutes to get there, park my clattering PT, and make it to the room. But my fee for this kind of translation is twice what it is for teaching, well worth the effort.

"It'll be tight, but I can make it."

On the way I pass Spago, a fancy Beverly Hills restaurant. A black Mercedes is parked on the corner. I can make out the driver, but only from the back. Briefly I find myself wondering if the man behind the wheel, whom I can see only in silhouette, might be Ray Patrick.

Cedars-Sinai is a sprawling complex, but I manage to get to Room 517 five minutes before the scheduled consultation. The patient appears to be around twenty years old. I introduce myself in French, but she answers in English, then tries to speak English until it becomes obvious that she can't. After that we speak only French. She has come to LA because she is much taken with American film stars. She has always wanted to see the city in which so many of them live. It is a short vacation. She must be back in Lyon by the middle of the month in order to resume her job as a cashier.

I ask her which movies stars are her favorites. She names Jennifer Lawrence and Bradley Cooper, both of whom are *"des grands artistes."* She wants to be an actress, but not in France.

French movies are boring. French actors are snobs.

The doctor arrives. He is short, with thinning hair, an appearance that reminds me of Mehdi. I can't help but wonder if he has secreted a Burger King crown.

I ask him to speak in brief phrases then pause long enough for me to translate.

He nods and begins.

An X-ray has revealed a tumor in Delphine's brain. Whether malignant or benign cannot be determined without surgery. She will need to consult a neurosurgeon as soon as she returns to France.

I pass on this news in as calm a voice as I can manage given how frightening it is.

Delphine is dazed and uncomprehending, as if hit by a hammer. She blinks slowly. Her lips part slightly. She is trying to absorb this terrifying news.

I turn to the doctor.

"Can you tell her something else?"

I want him to say something hopeful, or at least less horrifying. This diagnosis has taken so much from Delphine; some shred of hope must be given back.

He only stares at me gravely.

"She needs to have this surgery right away. As soon as she gets back to France."

The size of Delphine's tumor is in the doctor's

eyes. He has not told her more because the "more" is worse.

The tumor is probably malignant, he tells me with a glance, and if it is, twenty-year-old Delphine will be dead within a few months.

I look at her. "*Tu dois te faire opérer dès que possible.*" You must have an operation as soon as possible. And because it seems called for, I add, "*Immédiatement.*" Immediately.

Delphine's eyes fill with tears, but she doesn't speak. She'd no doubt imagined her life as more or less unending. She would have long, delightful years ahead of her. Time to fall in love, have adventures, achieve fame in the movies. Now that future has been derailed.

She reaches up to touch the side of her head. Her fingers are trembling.

"*Si tu veux, je peux rester avec toi,*" I tell her. If you want, I can stay with you.

"*Oui, ce serait bien,*" she says. "*J'ai besoin de toi.*" Yes, that would be nice. I need you.

Later I go to my car, but I don't start the engine. My nerves are on edge, death terribly real again, as if everything is shadowed by oblivion. I think of how briefly we live in time before we rejoin eternity.

Where Max is.

Where Melody is.

Then I think of Emma.

I have so little time to stop Simon.

110

But how?

What next?

I have written to him. There would be no point in doing that again.

Have I already reached a dead end, or just taken the last reasonable step?

Does that leave only an unreasonable one?

I can't step back from the precipice of this question, and yet I must face it:

What are you willing to do?

I yearn for someone to show me the way. As if searching for that person, I stare out into the garage. People are moving in and out of it. People in lab coats. People in wheelchairs. Some of them glance toward me.

What they see is a woman sitting motionless behind the wheel.

Still.

Very still.

If someone painted me now, I would look lonely, isolated.

Because I am.

The full realization of this falls upon me. More than anything, I want someone simply to believe me. Someone who can see the same threat and feel the same peril. A friend.

2.

After my last client, I decide to go by the pier before heading home. There's no reason for this except that I feel a need to acknowledge the young girl who drowned here. It is a distant gesture of respect, I realize, but it is . . . something.

On the boardwalk the mood is lively, as always. Tourists wander from booth to booth, playing games. Couples stroll with their arms around each other. I stop to watch a clown in a flaming red wig. He is blowing gigantic bubbles into the air. Children chase them and scream with delight when one bursts. Melody once had the same excitement. Dashing around. Eager to explore. On this same pier, when she was older, Simon and I watched as she strolled over to buy a cotton candy. "She takes my breath away," he said.

I keep walking until I glance to the side and see a yellow tent. Several police officers are in the process of taking it down. I watch as a woman joins me at the railing. She is tall, slender, dressed in a gray jogging suit. She peers out over the beach, her gaze focused on the cops as they continue to dismantle the tent.

Suddenly she turns to me.

"Did something happen on the beach?" she asks. "All those cops."

"They found a girl in the water yesterday," I tell her. "She hasn't been identified yet."

The woman looks back toward the beach.

"Water," she says. "I've always had a fear of it."

She looks at me almost playfully, as if dismissing this anxiety.

"No reason for it at all. I've had it since I was a little girl. It was worse back then. I didn't even want to take a bath. Now I can swim. But I never get over my head."

"Sounds like you're not really afraid of water," I tell her. "You're afraid of drowning."

"Yes, I guess that's it."

She laughs at this inexplicable anxiety, but I can feel her residual dread. It isn't in her voice. It's in her eyes.

Suddenly she seems to shy away from revealing anything more about herself.

"I wonder if she was from the streets," she says. "The girl they found."

She pulls her gaze back to the beach.

"They get hurt a lot, those girls."

"Yes, I know. I mentor a girl who was once like that. It's a hard life."

I sense that I've just sparked something in her mind.

"You said the girl you mentor once lived on the street?" she asks.

"Yes."

"She doesn't live on the street anymore?"

"That's right."

"How long has she been off the streets?"

"A year."

"How old is she?"

"Nineteen."

"And she's doing okay now?"

"Yes. She's doing fine. She has a regular job. An apartment."

The woman offers her hand. "I'm Julie Cooper."

"Claire Fontaine."

"When you mentioned this girl you're mentoring, it struck a chord, because I'm a freelance writer and I've been thinking of writing an article about girls who once lived on the street but have managed to get their lives back on track. Do you think the girl you mentor would be willing to talk to me?"

"I don't know, but I can ask her."

"Okay. In case she's willing, let me give you my number."

I take out my phone and add Julie Cooper's number to my contacts. "I'll let you know," I assure her.

She glances toward the Ferris wheel, then back to me.

"I'd better be going."

She smiles.

"I hope to hear from you. And by the way, you can call anytime. I stay up late."

When she walks away, I turn, look out over the water, and think again of the dead girl.

Though I have no idea what happened to her, I wonder what evidence might have been washed from her body as she rolled in the sea.

Are there bite marks that can no longer be distinguished as human? Bruises that might have been inflicted by driftwood?

Does whatever identification she might have had now lie buried in a grave of silt?

Will she forever be just another *inconnue*?

3.

Once at home, I call Destiny.

We chat idly for a while before I get to the reason for my call.

"I was on Santa Monica Pier this afternoon," I tell her. "I met a woman there. A writer. She's doing a story about girls who've managed to get their lives back. She'd like to talk to you."

Destiny is instantly suspicious.

"Why were you at the pier?" she asks.

"I don't know. I was just thinking about the girl in the water."

This only heightens Destiny's alarm.

"I didn't have anything to do with that girl."

"Of course not. The article isn't about the girl. It would be about you. And other girls like you. Girls who've gotten off the street."

Now Destiny is interested.

"So I'd be like a . . . source?"

"Yes."

She warms to the idea.

"My name in print? Wow."

She sounds like an actress who has just landed a major part.

I tell her that I'll make contact with the writer.

"Wow," Destiny repeats. "Me in an article."

We spend the rest of the conversation talking about whatever pops into Destiny's mind, though it's clear that she is already considering what she might say to the writer.

When the conversation is over, I make a quick dinner, read awhile, then go to my bedroom.

I have only one print on the wall over my bed. In the painting, a woman dressed in black lies facedown on a sofa. She is clearly overcome with grief and guilt. It is Jean Béraud's *Après la Faute*, a title usually translated as "After the Misdeed."

I hear the *ting* of an incoming email.

The sender calls himself the Watchman.

His message is: *Watching you.*

A streak of fear races through me.

This must be Simon's next move.

I hit the Reply button and write back.

I won't let you do it again.

I grow tense as I wait for the Watchman to reply. I feel his cyberfingers reaching for me, probing me without being seen.

But no *ting* comes.

His silence stokes my fear.

It's one of his tactics, part of his strategy.

He knows it will unnerve me.

And it does.

As the minutes pass, I begin to feel Simon everywhere, eyeing everything. I think of my Facebook page, my ads on Yelp, Thumbtack, Craigslist. He can see the paintings I post on

Pinterest. Perhaps he can do more than that. Has he found some hacker who can trace my purchases, find what books I'm reading, what songs I listen to, read my emails, my text messages?

I suddenly envision Simon in possession of all this information, thinking of how he can use it against me.

Crazy Claire compulsively watches the Femme Fatale Network.

Crazy Claire repeatedly buys books about men who abuse women.

Crazy Claire posts paintings of drowned girls.

I can't bear the thought of how deranged I can be made to seem.

I close my computer, then check the doors, the windows. All locked.

I resist the urge to keep a light burning in every room, because I imagine Simon somehow being aware of this, eager to report it.

Crazy Claire never turns off the lights.

I switch them off and sit in the darkness.

For some reason, I think of the woman on the pier.

It is late, but she'd said I could call her anytime.

I pick up my phone and tap out her number.

I feel strangely comforted when she answers immediately.

SLOAN

MY WORKDAY ENDED just after six.

On the way home I passed the Home Plate Bar, a favored LAPD watering hole. Nick Devine was just getting out of his car. He'd retired nearly ten years ago and was now living comfortably on a full pension, despite the fact that there wasn't a shady deal in LA he hadn't known about and profited from. He'd never owned a credit card, my father said, because he'd paid for everything with wads of cash collected from drug lords and corrupt contractors. He'd skimmed money from stolen-car rings, loan-sharking operations, anywhere a buck could be grabbed from a dirty hand.

From behind the wheel I watched as he got out of his car and strolled toward the entrance to the Home Plate. I knew that inside, he and his cronies would be laughing and high-fiving each other, retired cops who'd been no better than crooks.

During my time in the department, I'd seen cops gradually go wrong. I knew it started with a small gift. Not much at all. Just a little expression of appreciation. After that they went along with the other offers that came in. They told themselves that it wasn't bribery or a payoff. So what if you get a little help with the mortgage each month? Over time the fees and services got more serious. Because they took more, they had to give more. Before long they were doing things they'd never dreamed of when they were in the academy or a rookie on the street. That was what my father had always warned me against. Not some outright larceny that comes on suddenly, like accepting a big-money bribe, but the small ones that take little bites out of you every day, continue month by month and year by year, corroding you slowly, steadily, like rust.

I had always been watchful with regard to these small failures.

What I didn't know, and hadn't yet learned, was that temptation doesn't always come from the outside. There are weaknesses within, like a house built on an unsteady foundation and thus vulnerable to collapse.

At home, I felt my father's absence once again. The chair he'd sat in was empty. There was one plate on the table at dinner. At the grocery, I no longer bought his little treats: butter cookies, White Castle cheeseburgers he popped into the microwave. I no longer heard the creak of the floor beneath his feet, the clattering sound he made when he pulled up the blinds in the morning. All of that was gone.

What was left now?

My cases.

I turned on my computer and went to work.

There is an array of techniques for making people stop what they are doing, and the first of LA's sin eaters had generally relied on old Mob methods of intimidation. They'd put a dead rat in the mailbox. If that didn't work, the subject might come home and find the china cabinet overturned, sofas and mattresses cut open, clothes slashed. If there was a pet, it would be found dead in the kitchen sink. These men were thugs through and through, and they'd had a thug's lack of imagination.

My preferred approach was to play the good cop. I'd make my subjects think that I'd come over to their side, or at least understood their grievances. If they thought they'd been treated badly, I'd pretend to agree with them. *Yes,* I'd say, *you have a right to be angry. You have a right to want revenge, or at least compensation for all you've had to put up with. But you have to be reasonable,* I'd tell them. *If you want too much, you'll end up getting nothing.*

Claire Fontaine's case was a different story. She'd never asked Miller for money. She didn't want to bankrupt him. She wanted to destroy his reputation. If she continued on this path, I had no doubt that she'd leave nothing but ruin in her wake. Just like my mother had.

It was nearly midnight when my phone rang. I glanced at the caller ID and knew that at least the first aspect of my plan was working.

"Hello."

"Julie? It's Claire Fontaine. We met on the pier this afternoon."

I faked Julie's bouncy, energetic voice.

"Oh, yes. Claire, how are you?"

"I hope it's not too late to call, but you said I could do it anytime."

"Absolutely. What's up?"

She told me that the girl she mentored was willing to speak with me. She added a few details. Her name was Destiny, and she'd bounced around a little before ending up on Venice Beach.

We arranged to meet at a restaurant tomorrow afternoon.

It was an approach I'd used many times before. You slip into another identity, then insinuate yourself into your mark's life. With this call, I knew I could pull off this deception once again, because on the pier I'd sensed that Claire was lonely. She needed someone to whom she could tell her deepest, darkest thoughts. When people reach that point, you can draw them out as you draw them in.

First, though, I had to insure that no matter what I did or who I became, Claire would trust me. With that in mind, I got right to work.

I printed a card with Julie Cooper's name, phone number, and email address.

After that I thought through other elements of this new identity, considering the best way to approach Destiny. I came up with a way to get her attention and created a photo file on my phone for just that purpose. I even rehearsed what Julie Cooper would say or do to make sure I could do it smoothly and casually. I couldn't be an actress playing Julie, stumbling over lines, forgetting aspects of the part. I had to *be* Julie Cooper.

Last, I needed to plant a loaded item within the conversation I was going to have with Destiny. A detail that would prove that I was acquainted with the street life of the city. That's when I came up with Vicki Page, a woman I'd dealt with several times as a cop and whom I thought Destiny might have run into during her time on Venice Beach. Once Destiny knew I'd heard of Vicki, she'd figure I was a legit reporter.

By the time I'd completed the work of identity transformation, I felt certain that I had all the elements in place.

Destiny would fall for it.

Most important, so would Claire.

I was quite confident that very soon I'd be her best friend.

PART III

CLAIRE

WHEN I ARRIVE at my father's apartment, he is sitting on the balcony, watching hummingbirds swoop around their feeder. He is in his late seventies but looks older. There is a drawn quality to his face. A suppressed anger seeps from him.

I hand him the doughnuts.

"Snowies?" he asks before he opens the box.

His tone is vaguely doubtful, as if I have more than likely failed to bring him the type of doughnut he prefers.

"Snowies, yes," I tell him.

A few months after my mother died, he met Rose. Considerably younger. Full of energy. He called her his "firecracker." They dated for a year, and the whole time he was besotted with her. He wanted to marry her, but she hated kids. That's how I became his ball and chain.

He takes out one of the doughnuts and bites into it like an animal, tearing at it with his teeth. He is always this way, vaguely snarling.

He finishes his one doughnut and closes the cardboard lid over the rest. "Always save something for later, Claire."

He has forever given me precisely this kind of fatherly advice: I should buy, not rent. Penny saved, penny earned. You can't spend yourself rich.

"Still no man in your life?" he asks in the tone of an accusation, as if I am too crazy to love. Still, he wants me to find a man, a husband.

His smile is oddly mirthless.

"You'll meet someone," he says in a way that makes it clear he doesn't think my prospects are particularly good.

This is the same man who still considers Simon a "real find," a rich man I should never have accused of anything, "since you only had Melody's word."

Melody's word.

He never believed her either.

Sometimes I imagine Simon and my father in league with each other. Sitting in some bar together, plotting how to bring me to my senses. My father soothing Simon's frayed nerves, commiserating with him, even apologizing for my "problems."

He wipes away the white flecks left by the snowy by raking his right arm across his mouth. Swiftly. Roughly. Almost violently. Nearly all his physical movements have this frenzy. As if he is frantically cleaning up a murder scene. Wiping away prints. Mopping up blood.

After he tried to drown me, I never stopped being afraid of him. I cringed when he put his arms around me and held my breath until he released me. Each time he let me go, it felt like a stay of execution. The one time I confronted him about the boat, he flew into a rage. *Are you still nursing that stupid crap!* I was fifteen, and his explosive reaction frightened me, silenced me. I never mentioned it again.

"What's new?" he says.

I don't tell him about Simon's marriage plans, and certainly nothing about the letter I wrote to him. If I did, it would only confirm my father's certainty that I am hopelessly deranged. He has spent his life denying what he did. This must surely make him feel that he and Simon are mutual victims of my delusions.

Why do I see him, bring him snowies?

There is no good answer to that question.

Perhaps it's because I have never given up on some sort of reconciliation, a confession that would unburden his heart and open mine to him. This feeling reminds me of a painting I once saw on the streets of Paris. A tiny white egg in the palm of an enormous hand. The gigantic fingers are violently drawing in, and the egg seems almost to shrink in anticipation of being crushed. It was called *Hope.* My hope that my father will one day admit what he did is that frail egg.

"How's the teaching coming along?" my father asks. "You have plenty of clients?"

"Never plenty, but there are enough."

"You should teach online instead of being in your car all day."

His confidence that he is always right comes across as a kind of bluster. "Driving from place to place takes up too much time and cuts down on the profit," he adds.

His tone is almost scolding, as if I should have figured this out long ago. "It's better to do everything on your computer. Isn't that what people do now?"

"Some do."

"Why don't you?"

"I like personal contact," I tell him.

"Hm," my father grunts.

He shrugs, because once again I've rejected his generously offered paternal counsel.

"Well, it's your business, not mine."

We've spent our lives keeping our distance from each other. In his eyes, I am still the "frightened little bird" he used to call me each time I shrank away from him.

I stay a little while longer with my father, then leave.

The text bell rings as I reach my car.

It's from Phil.

Liked your response. Thought about it. Would still like to meet you. Understand if you say no. Just felt like trying.

Trying. The word touches me.

I want to answer him. Perhaps meet him for

coffee. But my world is too complicated now. I don't know what Simon may do next. Nor what I will do in response. My life no longer seems entirely my own. Certainly not one I should pull someone else into. I don't answer Phil's text, but I don't delete it, either. It seems strange to me that simply leaving his message on my phone feels like an act of faith.

2.

Ray is waiting at the same table as before.

He stands as I come forward.

"Good morning," he says brightly.

I sit down and begin to take out my materials.

Ray watches me silently.

There is a certain intensity in his gaze that makes me fear that Ava has told him more about me than she should have. Does he think I'm weak? Pathetic? Bitter? Crazy? Just having these questions makes me feel paranoid, though I know that I have not descended into madness. It isn't everyone I fear or distrust, after all. It is only Simon.

I notice that Ray is looking at my hands.

When he sees this, he quickly catches himself.

"Oh, sorry," he says. "I just saw that you don't have a wedding ring."

"I'm divorced."

"Do you mind if I ask whether you have children?"

He laughs before I can answer.

"I mean, since I'm at a child's level in French, I thought a woman who's had children might be more patient with me."

"I had a daughter."

The *had* registers gravely in his eyes. A daughter in the past tense.

I know that such a statement requires at least a small explanation.

"She died," I tell him. "Five years ago."

Abruptly my past, present, and future all seem to lie as if in ghostly pentimento beneath the image of Melody on the boat, standing in the rain, speaking hesitantly but resolutely. *Mom, I have to tell you something.*

"I'm sorry," Ray says.

He doesn't ask for more details and clearly regrets what he'd earlier thought to be a quite ordinary question.

There is an awkward silence while we both look for ways to change the subject.

I take the nearest to hand.

"How about you?" I ask as cheerfully as I can.

"Divorced. But I have a lovely daughter. Her name is Jade. She's eight years old."

He says nothing more about his daughter, and I add no further information about Melody.

I begin the lesson and it goes smoothly. Even during these brief exchanges, his accent improves.

When the hour ends, it seems to have passed very quickly.

Ray again appears to have more energy than when it began.

"It works like an exercise for my whole brain," he tells me cheerfully.

I fall back on a professional response.

"That's true. Studies show that learning a language improves all the cognitive skills. I know that sounds like part of a sales pitch, but it's true."

"Well, you don't have sell me," Ray says. "I'm convinced you're the right person for me."

I'm flattered by what he just said, but I keep my growing attraction to him carefully in check.

Love once felt easy.

But as Ray leaves and I pack up my materials, I think of Simon and wonder if anything will ever be easy for me again.

3.

Simon is still on my mind as I head for my car.

I know this is crazy, but I can't help thinking of him lurking behind some hidden nook or following me from a distance. I am trapped by his ubiquity, the way his presence, or the dread of it, pervades everything. I can't stop thinking about what he is and what he is going to do. He surrounds me like an acrid odor. I feel him as a sharp tingling in the air.

I stop, take a deep breath, and try to pull myself together.

I don't want to be like this.

Listening for footsteps behind me.

Catching my breath as cars approach.

Imagining Simon all around me.

As if he is a shape-shifter, able to assume different forms.

I remind myself that I am not deranged, not delusional. *Steady, Claire,* I tell myself. *Control yourself.*

I manage to walk unhurriedly toward my car, but I glance about continually. Left. Right. Behind me.

I feel myself becoming a different person.

Inhabited by Simon. As if I am his changeling.

Simon is winning.

I know this because I hesitate before reaching for the ignition key.

When I finally turn it, the engine fires to life. I feel relief when the car doesn't explode.

The phone rings just as I reach my next client. It's Ava.

"Simon called me," she says.

I'm stunned that he has done this. Ava has been my best friend for ten years, but she had little to do with Simon while we were married and has had nothing at all since the divorce. How desperate he must be to have called her. I feel as if the temperature has suddenly risen, the storm closer, its deadly lightning much nearer to me now.

"When did he call?"

"Five minutes ago. He says you threatened him, Claire."

"I warned him."

"Warned? Threatened? What's the difference?"

"They're completely different."

"Not really," Ava insists. She is clearly annoyed. "Not really, Claire," she repeats.

For her this is just a matter of semantics. The bottom line is that I have foolishly and impulsively gotten myself into big trouble.

"What did Simon say to you?" I ask her.

"He claims you've had some kind of break-down."

"That's ridiculous."

"Ridiculous or not, he's afraid of you. Of what you might do. He actually mentioned that you have a gun."

"You're kidding!"

"Do you have a gun, Claire?"

"It's Max's old gun. We used to go to a firing range in the desert. It was . . . recreational."

"But you still have it—that's my point."

I realize that Simon is coming across as the one who tells the truth, I the one who slants it.

He is the straight line.

I am the twisting one.

I have to restore my credibility.

"That gun stays in a locked drawer, Ava," I tell her insistently. "I haven't seen it for years."

"Well, all I can say is that you're freaking Simon out."

"Well, he can go—"

"Here's the rule, Claire," Ava interrupts. "The ex's future marriage is out of bounds. As a matter of fact, everything in his life is out of bounds. You have to say to yourself, 'He lives on Mars now. I have nothing to do with him.' "

When I offer no argument she plunges ahead.

"By the way, why didn't you tell me you'd called him? No, even better, why didn't you tell me before you did it?"

The answer is that she would have tried to talk me out of it, and I'd feared she might succeed.

"I had to do it," I reply weakly. "Emma is—"

"Out of bounds, that's what Emma is!" Ava cries. "You want to help a kid, give to UNICEF. What you don't do is stick your nose into Simon Miller's business a full five years after you divorced him."

I want to throw my phone out the window or smash it against a concrete wall.

"The whole system is on his side, Claire," Ava adds pointedly. "Accept it. He will get what he wants. Men like Simon always do."

Something cracks in me.

"I have to go."

I hang up just as Ava begins to speak again.

For a time I sit behind the wheel, peering at the phone, half hoping Ava will call back.

She doesn't, but a few minutes later I hear the *ting* of a message.

I pull over to read it.

At first there are no words.

It is only a photograph.

In extreme close-up.

Of two darkly staring eyes that seem to grasp for me, like talons.

There is a flashing violence in them, a sense of swooping down.

They are the eyes of a predatory bird.

Beneath them, two words.

Written in Satanic script, like a message sent from hell.

Once again he has found me.

The Watchman.

4.

Of course I say nothing about the eyes of the Watchman when I meet Destiny at 24/7 at the end of her shift.

The restaurant is almost empty now. Destiny calls it her "home away from home." Cal, the manager, provides meals as part of her salary and makes no effort to eject her from her favored booth as long as business is slow.

I have told her very little about Simon or Melody.

We talk about her desire to leave Los Angeles. She doesn't know where she wants to go. "Just somewhere else," she says.

The waitress arrives.

She puts my soup in front of Destiny and Destiny's cheeseburger in front of me.

"Anything else?"

"No, thanks," Destiny says.

She switches our plates as Muriel rumbles heavily back toward the kitchen.

"See what I mean?"

Her expression conveys complete disdain.

"It's not just that she's fat. It's that she's stupid."

Destiny takes a bite from her burger.

"Thrice cursed. That's what my tenth-grade teacher used to say. 'That girl is thrice cursed.' Meaning three of 'em."

She takes a sip of diet soda.

"That's Muriel. Fat. Dumb."

When Muriel's third curse doesn't immediately occur to her, she gives up with a shrug.

"Anyway, fat and dumb."

I glance out into the parking lot, my gaze alert to black SUVs. There aren't any.

"What's her name again?" Destiny asks.

I turn to her. "Who?"

"The writer."

"Julie. Julie Cooper."

"Is she, like, old?"

"About my age, I guess. Early forties. If you think that's old, then yes, she's old."

To keep the conversation going, I ask, "When you meet her, do you want me to hang around, or would you rather I leave?"

Destiny ponders the question as if it's philosophical.

When she makes up her mind, she shrugs.

"You can stay," she says. "It doesn't matter."

Nothing really matters to Destiny. There is a lack of will that makes me wonder if she is in fact a fit subject for Julie's article. She was more or less plucked off the street and deposited in a center for homeless young women. Social workers found her a job and a place to live. She has done little but follow the rules they laid down. I detect no interest in taking the wheel of her own life. I fear that the slightest nudge in the wrong direction will send her over the cliff.

I turn back toward the parking lot. I am still peering out the window when Julie pulls up.

"She's here," I tell Destiny.

Destiny straightens. "Shit."

Suddenly she's jumpy.

"What's wrong?" I ask her.

"I don't know," Destiny answers. "A reporter. It makes me nervous."

"There's nothing to worry about."

"Unless it's a cover. Her being a reporter, I mean."

"A cover for what?"

"Maybe she's a cop."

This is ludicrous. I wave my hand dismissively. "Relax, Destiny."

Outside, Julie is walking toward the restaurant. Her stride is confident, almost bold. She is the opposite of me. At home in the open space, in the sunlight. I can't imagine her world, how unburdened it must be.

"We all made it here," she says brightly when she comes up to our booth. "Hi, Claire."

"Hi."

She looks at Destiny and smiles cheerfully.

"Happy to meet you," she says.

Destiny is unprepared for such an upbeat greeting.

"Thanks," she says cautiously.

Julie is dressed in a pantsuit. Her blouse is white with a broad collar. She gives off a stylish professionalism.

"Well, thanks for seeing me," she says as she takes a chair opposite Destiny. "I appreciate it."

To break the ice, I say, "Destiny thought you might be an undercover cop."

Julie laughs. "Not me. No way. But my dad was a cop. Back in the day, he would take me to the station, introduce me as 'the crop.' By that, he meant that I was his only child. And my God, that station house. The atmosphere inside it was so male. Decades of testosterone embedded in the walls. It covered them like paint. You could almost smell it."

She laughs again.

"Now there are a lot of women cops. But back then? All those old, sweaty guys? It completely put me off following in my dad's footsteps."

She sits back and crosses her arms casually. "Destiny, I hear you have a job and a place to live."

"Yeah."

"That's awesome."

"I guess."

"Don't guess," Julie says forcefully.

She whips out her phone, taps an icon, and turns the phone toward Destiny and me.

The picture is of a dead young woman sprawled in an alley.

As Destiny watches, Julie flips through an assortment of dead-girl pictures. They lie beneath bridges, in ditches, stuffed into storm drains. Most of them are either naked or half-naked. Only one is fully clothed. They have been shot, stabbed, bludgeoned, strangled.

Destiny looks at each girl in turn, but nothing seems to register in her mind. These dead girls might as well be bits of scattered rubbish.

Julie flips to the final photograph in her collection.

"This is the latest one," she tells Destiny. "I snapped it from the online *LA Times* this morning. The police don't know who she is, so they're asking the public for information."

I stare at the photo on Julie's phone.

It is the face of a girl in her teens. One eye closed, the other half open, filmy. Perhaps it had once been blue. Her lips are slightly parted, enough to reveal her teeth. The shape of her mouth reminds me of Camille Monet, painted on her deathbed, in a swirl of blankets that are strangely mobile, flowing around her like water.

"They found this girl floating near Santa Monica Pier," Julie says.

She looks at Destiny significantly. "Do you

know why I wanted to show you these pictures?"

Destiny shakes her head.

"Because any one of these girls could have been you," Julie says.

I take this to be a journalistic shock tactic, something to light a fire in Destiny. Julie is giving her a powerful representation of what her future might have been if she had remained on the street.

It appears to work.

Destiny's eyes widen as she stares at the last of the photographs.

At first she seems riveted by the image, but as she continues to look at the photograph, a different reaction emerges. I can tell that she is in the midst of some sort of calculation, a balancing of possibilities. She is like someone at a fork in the road, deciding which one to take.

This argument lasts only a couple of seconds. Then she blinks all this away, one of the roads at last chosen.

"I've seen this girl," she says. "She was always hanging around the beach. Painting pictures. She had a little wooden easel she dragged around with her. And a little stool—the kind that folds up—to sit on."

I am astonished to hear this. "What did she paint?" I ask.

"Whatever was in front of her. The beach. Palm trees. She did it early in the morning. To keep from getting caught. But it wasn't graffiti she was painting. Gang names, space creatures, that kind of shit. It was more a real picture."

"Of what?"

"A house. But it looked weird. Like it was about to fall down."

There is another pause before she adds, "She painted it on a cement wall. On Venice Beach. Over by McDuffy's."

"Did she sign it?" I ask.

Julie looks at me quizzically.

"In the news, it says she hasn't been identified," I explain. "But if she signed her painting, then the cops would at least have her name."

Julie smiles. "You should have been a cop, Claire."

Without further prompting Destiny launches in to a full report on the girl in the water.

She didn't know her well, she tells Julie, but she saw her quite often, always on Venice Beach. She has no idea of the girl's identity or where she came from. She remembers that the girl seemed friendly, though she never spoke. She was always painting. She never did street portraits and never painted for money. In fact, she'd given her paintings to anyone who wanted them. She'd even given a few of them to Destiny.

Julie looks at Destiny intently.

"You know, those girls on the beach can fall in with some pretty bad people," she says.

Destiny is abruptly on alert again. Julie's question has warned her of some subtle change of direction.

"It's a beach," she says. "Crowded. Yeah, sure, you get to know people. And yeah, some of them aren't nice."

"My contacts in the LAPD tell me that a lot of the street girls around Venice Beach get picked up by a woman named Vicki Page."

Destiny's eyes darken, but she says nothing.

"Ever heard of her?" Julie asks.

Destiny says nothing.

"She's pretty well known in that part of town," Julie adds. "By the street people, I mean. And the cops, of course. I thought you might have run across her."

Destiny shrugs.

"Is that a yes or a no?" Julie asks. "About Vicki?"

"I've heard of her, yeah—just the name."

"Okay, no problem," Julie says.

She clicks off her phone, and the image of the girl in the water vanishes. "Okay," she repeats as she takes a pen and notebook from her bag. "Tell me about how you managed to get off the street."

I can see that Destiny wants to impress Julie with how tough and resourceful she is. She reveals a little more to her than she has to me, but her story remains sketchy. She's "bounced around" a lot and has had a long list of "crappy" jobs. Cleaning horse stalls. Spinning signs. Dressing monkeys for the circus, which, she says, is the hardest job on earth, " 'cause those little bastards hate wearing clothes."

She looks at me with a slight smile.

"I never told you about the monkeys, did I, Claire?" she asks.

From there she relates a tale of whirlwind adventure. Moving from city to city. Harrowing experiences with men and weather. The daily ordeal of finding a place to sleep. A catalogue of makeshift refuges: storm drains, tunnels, large cardboard boxes, sheets of plastic. During her life on the road, she has known them all.

There is a definite bravado in the way Destiny presents herself. She is the heroine of the tale. Always escaping narrowly. She wants Julie to believe that she is clever. That she has always outsmarted everyone else.

Julie listens to her closely, taking in the details, but something in her gaze tells me she's not buying it. Even so, she remains patient, giving Destiny free rein to unfold the saga of her life in whatever way she chooses.

At last Destiny winds her way closer to the present. To my surprise she credits others with what she calls her "salvation." Social workers. Counselors.

"And Claire, of course," she says toward

the end of this chronicle. "Claire's the best."

Julie's eyes slide over to me.

"Absolutely," she says with a quick wink. "The best."

For the next few minutes, I watch as Destiny continues her story.

As she talks, she grows more relaxed.

It's obvious that Julie has gained her confidence by keeping the tone light and conversational despite the grim subject matter. Julie never judges Destiny. She does not criticize her.

After a while Destiny is talking about the darkest aspects of her life in a way that seems to lift her spirits. With each revelation she becomes less burdened by her past.

I admire Julie's technique more and more as the interview continues. She is a wizard at conveying sympathy without indulging Destiny's tendency toward self-pity. She talks about how self-reliant Destiny is, and credits her with superior street smarts. With each compliment Destiny opens up a little more. They seem almost like older and younger sisters. It's a connection I have failed to establish with Destiny, and which I can't help but envy.

Julie glances at her watch. "Well, this has been terrific," she says enthusiastically. "You're a great source. I know you must be tired at the end of a working day. I won't keep you."

"Yeah, I better get out of my uniform."

"I hope you're willing to talk to me again," Julie adds.

"Sure," Destiny says. She smiles. "Any time."

Julie thrusts out her hand and Destiny takes it without hesitation.

"Thanks, Destiny," Julie says. "I'll be in touch."

After Destiny leaves, Julie returns her notebook to her bag, takes a sip from her coffee, looks at me.

"Well, that went well, don't you think?" she asks.

"Very well."

She smiles. "How did you meet Destiny?"

"She was more or less assigned to me."

"How long have you been mentoring her?"

"A year."

"Do you think she'll make it?"

"Make it?"

"To a better life."

"You mean, permanently?"

"Yes."

"I don't know."

For the first time Julie's vivaciousness drops away and I glimpse the serious woman beneath the charm.

"I guess it depends on what *better* means, doesn't it?" she asks. She suddenly looks at me very seriously. "Life sometimes takes us by surprise," she says. "You trust someone. You get betrayed. People you thought you knew turn out to be different. Things happen that you could never have expected or foreseen. Someone you thought was a saint turns out to be monster."

With this change of tone, Julie seems far more somber and knowing. Beneath her friendliness and vitality there is a troubled undercurrent not unlike my own.

"It shouldn't be this hard to get it right," she adds. "But it's easy for things to get fouled up."

She smiles, but it's the sad smile of a woman who has been disappointed.

In others.

In herself.

"And it's easy to blame yourself for it all. To feel you've screwed up. Made a big mess of everything. That it's all your fault for some crazy choice you made and now can't change or take back."

She shrugs.

"In the end, you become your own fall guy," she adds.

She looks at me as if we've both been derailed by some vast conspiracy, equal victims of a crime.

"And who wants to feel helpless?"

SLOAN

I SAW A spark in Claire's eyes when I said the word "helpless." My "saint turns out to be a monster" line had been an effective turn of phrase, too.

She probably wanted to talk a little longer, but I knew that now wasn't the right time. It was better to ease off, let things lie. If you push too hard, you risk the danger of exposing yourself. A paranoid is always on alert, always suspicious. I had to pace my approach to Claire perfectly or I'd tip my hand.

I didn't have forever, of course. If Miller was right, Claire would "do something" before his upcoming marriage. Even without that information, I could see an inner clock ticking in Claire Fontaine. There was an anxiousness beneath her reserve, a ferment. She was closing in on a grave deadline.

I looked at my watch again and pretended to be late for something.

"I'd better get going," I said.

Claire walked me out into the parking lot and over to my car.

"Thanks again for putting me in touch with Destiny," I told her.

Claire smiled. "I think she enjoyed the interview. The way you talked to her. She related to you."

She stood quite still, staring at me in a way that was almost imploring before she said, "Can I ask you a question?"

"Sure."

"Do you ever just . . . know something?"

"What do you mean?"

"That someone did something or is going to do something. Even though you don't have any proof."

I knew that for Claire, this wasn't an idle question. She put weight on it. My answer had to be right.

I thought fast and came up with a story my father had related to me about a woman named Stella Denker.

As I told it, I could almost see him on a dusty porch, a door opening to his knock, a woman facing him, her strained features captured in a slant of light.

A little boy named Charlie Fields had disappeared. My father had still been in uniform at the time, and he'd been given the job of going door to door in the kid's neighborhood.

He'd knocked several times before Stella had finally come to the door. She was tall and very thin, with dry, cracked skin.

He informed Stella why he was there. She said she'd heard about what she called "the missing kid." She didn't know the boy, however. She described herself as a shut-in but gave no indication as to why she never went out.

The door was slightly ajar, and while my father stood on the porch, he could see that it was stone dark inside. No lights burning. A stillness throughout the shadowy interior of the house.

"I ain't seen nothing," she told my father.

My father suspected something about Stella. Something . . . off. Unfortunately, with no proof he'd let the feeling slide and gone on to the next house.

Later that same day the body of Charlie Fields was found in the basement of Stella Denker's house. She'd tried to burn it down, but the firemen had arrived in time to put it out.

As it turned out, Stella had coaxed Charlie into her house because she was sick, weak, needed help. The idea was to use him pretty much as a slave. By the time the insanity of such a notion had dawned on her, Stella had already committed a long list of felonies. Kidnapping, to start with. She had to flee but couldn't take Charlie or leave him alive. She'd poisoned him with strychnine.

According to the coroner's report, Charlie had been dead for little more than an hour when the firemen arrived. This meant that he'd been alive when my father knocked on Denker's door. He may have heard my father's voice, and his young heart may have leaped with hope that the man would save him. Tragically, my father had ignored his instincts with regard to Stella Denker. As a result, Charlie Fields had died.

"Your father thought he was responsible for that little boy's death?" Claire asked at the end of my tale.

I nodded. "All his life."

This was actually true, though I made sure it seemed a darker burden than it had been. The point was to establish a foundation for future intimacy. Once the subject was broached, it could be explored later.

I smiled and offered Claire my hand.

"Call me anytime," I told her.

It was a ploy that further deepened our connection by letting Claire know that if she needed me, I'd be there for her. More important, it established that if I ever found myself in need, I could call her, too.

Mutual care.

It's important for a sin eater to realize that human beings like that sort of thing.

CLAIRE

I'M IN NO mood to see Mehdi, but I arrive at six p.m., right on time.

He welcomes me with an excited smile. "So happy," he says, "always."

He is dressed in Iranian style, a shirt that falls almost to his knees and trousers that look like puffed-out silk.

"Shirt is called *kurta*," he informs me brightly. "Pants called *dhoti*." He clearly expects me to appreciate traditional attire.

I smile thinly. "Very nice."

Mehdi's mood dims. "You don't like?" he says with a slight sulk.

"Okay, let's get started."

I recall the glass table.

"How about the living room?" I suggest.

Mehdi looks as if some subtle plan has been thwarted.

"Uh . . . well . . ." he sputters. "Yes, okay . . . living room."

The living room is large and luxurious.

I'm about to take a chair, but Mehdi directs me to an L-shaped sofa upholstered in dark red velvet. The angle of the sofa blocks me on the left, and there is a large table in front of me. I have the uneasy feeling that I have been corralled. I fight the sensation and stay put.

"Do you have the study sheets I gave you last time?" I ask.

Mehdi is wholly at a loss.

"The vocabulary list," I remind him. "And the present tense conjugations."

"Ah, yes . . . Can we?"

I look at him quizzically.

"Can we what?"

He spreads his feet slightly and places his fists at his sides, like a soldier at parade rest.

"I did something for you today, Claire."

He waits for me to ask what he did, but I say nothing.

"I got . . . clean."

I have no idea what he is talking about.

"Brazilian," he adds with a proud smile, as if recounting a tale of heroism. "Wax."

He clearly expects me to be pleased by this news.

"It hurt," Mehdi informs me. "But I know you like it."

He knows no such thing.

He takes my silence for encouragement and sweeps down beside me, blocking my only exit.

"All clean for you, Claire," he repeats. "All smooth. Soft as baby."

I point to a chair.

"Sit over there, Mehdi."

He looks hurt.

"You don't like Brazilian wax?"

"Sit over there."

He doesn't move.

"I know you have feelings for me," he says. It strikes me that he actually believes this. "And I have these same feelings for you, Claire."

His hand crawls across his lap to settle on his leg, which he presses lightly against mine.

"Stop, Mehdi."

I edge my leg away.

"Stop!"

He stares at me like a little boy denied a sweet.

"Claire," he says softly. "You know that I love you."

I want to leap up, but I fear that such a move might inflame him. He has dressed himself like a groom for me. He has gotten waxed for me. This is a man who has lost control of himself. It is up to me to control him. My next move will cause his next move. I must calculate them both.

"Mehdi. You are my client. Nothing more."

His hands curl into his lap and lie there like dead birds.

"I could give you so much, Claire," he says in a kind of croon. "Flowers every day. Beautiful jewelry. Beautiful like you. Anything you want."

His large, sad eyes take on the hollow ache of displaced longing.

"Caicos. Champagne."

I look at him sternly.

"Mehdi! Stop!"

He sees his horrible misstep.

"Oh, okay, so can we start again, Claire?"

He inches away from me.

"Can we forget and start again?"

A tiny smile flutters onto his lips.

"We just do French, okay?" he asks.

"All right," I answer calmly. "But not tonight. I don't want to have a class tonight."

Mehdi is now fully conscious of his dreadful miscalculation.

"Okay," he whispers.

He is hollowed out, stung with embarrassment.

Regardless of his retreat, I'm still not sure I should rise.

I let a beat pass, then another. With each ticking second, the bomb seems to defuse more safely.

I rise slowly.

"I'd better be going."

Mehdi sits in the same devastated posture, his head lowered.

I am standing over him now.

Peering down.

Waiting.

He stays in place, blocking my way.

"Mehdi, I need to get by."

He comes to life.

"Oh, sorry."

He quickly gets to his feet.

"I'll walk you to the door."

He steps aside and lets me pass in front of him, now careful not to touch me.

We walk together toward the door. There are small dots of perspiration on his brow. I also detect a smell. Cologne, but faintly sour.

He opens the door.

"Well. Goodnight, Claire."

I step into the evening air, then move down the stairs.

At my car, I look back. He has gone inside. The door is closed.

2.

After leaving Mehdi, I drive and drive.

I am shaken by his aggressiveness.

I need air.

The city's streets sweep by. I feel myself losing my connection to them. It's as if some part of me has already left Los Angeles, or that the city is now only a backdrop.

In order to ground myself, I decide to drive to Venice and look at the drowned girl's painting. Perhaps that will bring me down to earth again.

The painting is exactly where Destiny said it would be, on a large cement wall near McDuffy's.

Much of the wall is covered with the usual graffiti, but I see the house Destiny described. The windows are red squares and the door is black, like the mouth of a cave. There are some trees, all with dark brown trunks, thick green splotches for leaves. Also a shrub or two, mostly done in swirls of a somewhat deeper green. A pale road leads to the house. It is streaked with thin gray lines, by which the girl may have meant to suggest cracks of some sort. Beyond these markings there is little added detail. Nor is there any sense of perspective. The house, trees, shrubs, and even the road occupy the same flat surface.

She has little technique, but her work has a force that goes beyond artistic skill. It's raw and fierce, and there is something in it that grabs my attention, a crying out.

Her struggle fortifies me.

I return to my car and head toward home.

On the way a text comes in. I pull over to read it.

A telephone number, followed by a brief message: *If you change your mind.*

Phil.

It is almost ten when I reach home. I glance toward Mr. Cohen's house as if seeking a friend. Sometimes he sits on his front porch, but tonight he is not there.

Once in the house, I lock the door behind me, check the windows.

I find everything secure, then turn on the television.

The movie is called *Phantom Lady*, and in the opening scene a man and a woman meet in a bar. He has two tickets to a show, one of them for a woman who has jilted him. He asks the unknown woman to go with him. When she agrees, he starts to tell her his name, but she stops him cold. "No names and no addresses," she says. "Just companions for the evening." They leave in a taxi, and during the ride to the theater the woman suddenly becomes afraid of what she's done, the rash act of trusting a stranger. She tries to leave the cab, but the man stops her. There's nothing to fear, he assures her, they'll just have a few laughs. The woman's face is veiled in a strange, heart-breaking sorrow. "I'd like to laugh," she tells this unknown man. "It would be fun to laugh."

I know exactly how she feels.

I snap off the television.

I'm done with the Femme Fatale Network. It stokes my anxiety and fear. There are too many stories of victimized women. Women being deceived, cheated. Gaslighted. I think of poor, frantic Ingrid Bergman. Those jittery eyes. The flitting movement of her hands. She channels her husband's malice, is wholly distorted by his manipulation. No one will believe her. She is just another "frightened little bird."

I walk into my bedroom. I have no desire to sleep. I have slept very poorly since writing to Simon, and each encounter I've had with him has made any form of relaxation more difficult.

I know that tonight when I close my eyes, I'll see SUVs and muscular men in dark glasses.

Have I become the woman Simon has described to others and whom Dr. Lind diagnosed?

Yes, I have.

Because when my phone rings, I jump. My dread spikes as I glance at the phone and see Unknown Caller.

I stare at the phone.

When I finally pick it up, my hand is quivering. "Yes," I say in a flat voice.

"Hi, Claire."

"Destiny?"

"Yeah."

"Are you using a different phone?"

"Oh, shit. Yeah. It's a burn phone."

"Burn phone?"

"You know, a throwaway."

"Why do you have a—"

"Can I come over?" Destiny interrupts. "I really need to talk to you, Claire."

"Oh, okay," I tell her. "Come."

"Thanks. I'll be there in half an hour."

She arrives a few minutes later. "Hi," she says. She is tense. From her expression, I know that something's happened. There's been a turn. She's been thrown off course by it somehow.

"What's wrong?" I ask her.

She looks at me worriedly. "Do you think that writer is after me?"

"After you?"

"The way she stared at me. Like maybe I hurt that girl. I had nothing to do with her."

She says this with a fierce insistence, accustomed to having people doubt her stories.

"And those questions," she adds. "That stuff about Vicki Page. Like she suspected me of being connected to her."

"Nobody suspects you of anything," I assure her.

"You don't know her, right? You just met her."

"Yes."

"At the pier, like you said."

"At the pier."

Destiny glances toward the street, half expecting to see some sinister figure lurking melodramatically under the streetlamp. When she turns back toward me, her eyes glint like those of an anxious animal.

"Come inside," I say quickly.

She walks into my foyer warily, looking about like a cat suddenly put down in an unfamiliar setting, already looking for a place to hide.

I escort her to my living room.

"Look, Claire," Destiny says, "you've been really nice to me. I want to be straight with you. And the thing is, what I said to that writer, maybe I shouldn't have said some of that stuff, you know?"

Destiny's sudden change of attitude surprises me.

"I thought you liked Julie. You seemed to."

"Yeah, sure. She was okay, but . . ."

She hesitates before going on. She seems unsure of where to begin.

"The thing is, when she mentioned Vicki Page, whether I knew her or not, I said I didn't. Which isn't true. And shit, maybe she already knows I'm lying. She looked like she knew."

"Why did you lie?"

"Because if I told you I knew Vicki, she'd think I was one of her girls. But I don't do that."

She is briefly silent, gathering in the plot points.

"Vicki wanted me to work for her. Be one of her girls. She said it was easy money. I didn't care. I never did that, Claire."

I see an almost animal desperation in her eyes.

"And about that girl. Yeah, I knew her."

She yanks her backpack from the floor, unzips it, pulls out a few squares of cardboard, and thrusts them toward me.

"I brought these to show you."

They are watercolor renderings of various scenes. The first is a strangely violent seascape. The waters are boiling and the beach cringes, as if in anticipation of their assault. It has the same raw power as the house I saw earlier. Like that painting, it has an aura of impending destruction, of furious winds and tidal waves. The second is of a forest with trees that appear to have been ravaged by a storm. The third is a city street, the buildings leaning brokenly.

"Why did she give them to you?" I ask.

"She gave them to anybody who'd take them. It didn't matter who. I mean, it's not like I was a friend of hers."

When I try to hand the paintings back to Destiny, she refuses to take them.

"No, you keep them," she says. "I don't want them."

"Why not?"

"Because they could be, like . . . evidence against me."

"Evidence of what?"

"That I had something to do with her . . . which I didn't."

If I don't take these paintings, Destiny will simply toss them into the nearest dumpster. That would be an insult to the girl's memory, almost a sacrilege.

"Okay, sure," I tell her. "I'll take them."

Destiny is relieved.

"Thanks, Claire."

She fidgets nervously with the handle of her backpack.

"I'm spooked, that's all. By her knowing about Vicki Page."

She seems almost to be talking to herself, searching for a way to undo whatever mistake she thinks she has made.

"I should have just kept my mouth shut," she says finally.

She is now in full self-condemnation.

"Stupid. Stupid!"

She looks at me almost pleadingly.

"I just wanted to be in the paper, you know?

See my name in the paper. Be important for, like, five seconds. How screwed up is that?"

She shakes her head violently.

"Now I got this reporter on my tail."

This is an extreme reaction to her meeting with Julie. Something in it doesn't ring true.

"Do you know more about the girl in the water than you're telling me?" I ask.

"No," she answers vehemently. "No. I swear."

"Then there's nothing for you to worry about."

"You really think so?"

"Julie's just writing a story about girls who manage to get themselves off the street," I assure her. "She's not writing about the girl in the water or Vicki Page."

I touch her shoulder.

"Don't worry."

She calms slightly.

"Okay, Claire."

We talk for a few more minutes before Destiny decides to go home.

"I got the breakfast shift in the morning," she tells me.

I walk her to the door, then out to her car, a broken-down relic left behind by Time Warp, his parting gift to her.

She waves as she drives away.

At the end of the block, she turns to the right and disappears.

I walk back into my house.

I feel a need to check the windows and the doors again, but I force myself not to do it.

I also have an urge to call someone.

Just to hear another voice.

I think of Ava, then of Ray.

Even more, I think of Julie Cooper.

Our last conversation.

She'd seemed instinctively to understand my uneasiness and sense of helplessness. She was one of those people who didn't require everything to be explained. Her antennae were always out, probing the unsaid, the unseen.

Briefly I consider making that call, but I decide against it and turn on the television, using its steady drone and flashing images as a substitute for real companionship.

The movie is *In a Lonely Place*.

Humphrey Bogart is accused of something he didn't do. I watch for a while, then drift off to sleep, my body curled up on the sofa. I am still there when dawn breaks the next morning.

3.

It's almost as if Simon has shaken me awake, because the instant I open my eyes, I think of him.

I imagine him talking to fellow lawyers.

To judges.

To friends in the police.

I try to get rid of my fear that he really is invulnerable.

It's only the beginning of the day, but I already feel exhausted.

I sit alone in the building light.

I have a coffee.

Time passes.

It's nearly nine. I have thirty minutes before I meet Ray at Starbucks. I grab my bag and rush for the door.

Then I stop dead.

A huge spray of flowers rests on my doorstep. There must be two dozen of them, nestled in a thicket of tropical fern. Lilies. But rather than white, they are a dark, mournful color and hang heavily from their stalks, like a ragged shroud. Sinister. The flowers of death.

Is this Simon's next move?

Is this the way he intends to intimidate me?

A threat disguised as a peace offering?

He is laying the groundwork for his own defense. Trying to establish how kind he is, how conciliatory. I know better. This is just his latest ploy.

A white envelope is attached to one of the flowers. Simon has no doubt written some sweet sentiment.

I snatch the envelope from the flower and open it. The card inside is small, square, and the words I read are engraved.

Persian lilies for my Persian queen.
Mehdi.

I am shocked by how I instantly assumed the flowers were from Simon. My dread of him is distorting everything. Inflating everything. He would like nothing better than for me to become completely deranged. Cry out that he is watching me from behind the unlighted camera eye of my computer, listening to me through its tiny speakers.

In a parting nightmare vision, I imagine Simon viewing me on some remote screen, grinning fiendishly while I stare transfixed at the flowers.

I am still in the grip of this image when I arrive at Starbucks for my class with Ray.

"Good morning, Claire," Ray says when I reach his table.

I sit down in the chair opposite him. *"Bonjour."*

"Everything okay?"

"Yes, quite okay."

Since he is in the art business, I pattern the day's lesson to that field. I have made a list of art terms. My plan is to use them as a base for teaching him the rudiments of the language.

I hand him a sheet of French words: *Tableau. Peintre. Luminosité.*

"*La couleur*," I say. "The color."

He pronounces the word as if the final syllable is *ure*. I correct him, and he tries again. Still wrong. He tries again. This time it's better.

"*Très bien*, Ray."

We go to the next word, then the next. I try to keep focused, but I can't stop thinking about Simon.

When I look up from the worksheet, I find Ray regarding me closely. "You remind me of a portrait I saw in the Orsay," he says. "The one of Madame de Loynes. Do you know it?"

In fact I know this painting very well. While at the Sorbonne, I wrote an essay about it.

Madame de Loynes was a courtesan who later married a count. She's dressed elegantly in black, with long dark hair that hangs below her shoulders. Her skin is very pale and her features are delicate. She seems at home in herself. Peaceful. Secure. Nothing like me.

I tell Ray about my paper and how, as a young student, I'd been fascinated both by the portrait and by the woman.

"But I don't see any resemblance between Madame de Loynes and myself," I add.

"Not physically, no," Ray says. "But a critic who saw her portrait said she had both the world and the demimonde in her eyes. Sometimes you have that look. Your demimonde shows through."

"Frankly, I'd like to get rid of my demimonde."

"Me, too. I'd like to forget an unfaithful wife."

He waits for me to tell him a matching story, but for me, opening up is not an option. In fact, I hate it.

I reveal nothing about my life. After all, I am only his French teacher.

Instead I mention the girl in the water. He remembers hearing about her on television but hasn't followed the case.

I tell him that I have a few of her paintings.

"Did she have any talent?"

"Yes, she did."

"I'd like to see them."

This seems more than an idle remark.

"Why?"

"I have a little room in my gallery that I use to exhibit works that might otherwise go unnoticed. If she had some talent, I could give her work a little . . . show."

This strikes me as a very generous offer.

"Where are the paintings now?" Ray asks.

"At my house."

"Would you mind if I swung by and took a look?"

His interest in these paintings surprises me.

"Or you could bring them to my gallery if you prefer," he adds.

I wonder if I have given off some flicker of caution and distrust that makes him think I am hesitant to have him come to my house.

I don't want him to have this feeling, so I act quickly to ease his mind. "No, my house is fine."

Ray smiles. "Okay, when can I come over?"

"Tomorrow night?"

"Sure."

I give him the address, then immediately resume my role as French teacher.

"All right," I say. "Let's work a little with verbs."

I hand him a page that contains the present indicative conjugation for *chanter*, to sing.

"This is a regular verb," I tell him.

We go through the present tense of the verb.

Ray's recitation is halting at first, but eventually he speaks more fluidly and his pronunciation improves.

"Okay, now let's try an irregular verb," I say. "*Etre*. To be."

We go through the present-tense conjugation: *Je suis. Vous êtes. Il est.*

As Ray repeats after me, I find myself drawn to him, though I give no indication of this.

Instead I bring my attention back to the lesson.

And yet each time I look at him, I feel an odd charge.

The process of falling in love has always begun this way for me. Not as a tidal wave but as a soft rippling. In the past I greeted this feeling with pleasure and excitement. Now it's like a gift, beautifully wrapped, with a large bow, but which I can no longer accept.

4.

Ava is waiting at our usual table when I meet her for lunch. She is peering at me quizzically.

"Do I detect a little glow, Claire?" she asks.

"Maybe a tiny one," I admit.

She goes gossipy. "Let me guess. Ray Patrick?"

She's right. Still, I feel no need to rush into things. I play it down.

"We've only met three times. And just for lessons."

"When do you move to dinner and dancing?"

"I'm not sure we will."

"Why so hesitant?"

"My history."

"Which you have to put behind you, Claire."

I look at her determinedly. "I will. At some point."

Ava's expression is full of warning.

"Remember after that whole business with the hospital? I came to get you the day you were released. You should have seen yourself, Claire. You were half dead. You'd lost so much weight. You didn't laugh. You barely talked."

I pick up the menu.

"What are you going to have?" I ask.

176

"It's a salad for me," Ava answers. "I've declared war on my love handles."

The waiter appears. We order.

"Tell me something interesting," Ava says when he leaves.

I tell her the story of meeting Julie Cooper on the pier, then about Destiny's interview.

Ava focuses on what she considers the most relevant detail.

"Why were you at the pier?"

"To pay my respects."

"To what, that big Ferris wheel?"

"No. The drowned girl."

Ava is aghast.

"Why are you sticking your nose into something like this, Claire?"

"I'm not sticking my nose into anything. I just stopped by the pier and ran into this reporter. When it turned out she was writing an article about girls who'd managed to get off the street, I told her about Destiny. I liked her. We had a little talk as I was leaving. I think we have something important in common."

"Like what?"

"A feeling that you have to act. That you can't sit by and just let bad things happen. Not if you can prevent them."

Ava looks disturbed.

"You're talking about Simon, aren't you? About . . . stopping him."

She shakes her head with exasperation, abruptly changes the subject to a property she is showing later this afternoon. It has a heated pool and a bowling alley and once belonged to a film star of the forties.

I recognize the actress's name.

She was in a several noir films.

Blond.

Always smoking a cigarette.

With a sly look in her eyes.

I ask myself what such a woman would do in my place.

How far would she go to stop Simon?

Would she write another letter?

Make another call?

And if nothing worked and she remained convinced that he would do it again?

What then would she do?

The answer that comes to me is chilling.

She would kill him.

5.

I am heading to my last client of the day when my phone rings.

It's Mehdi.

"Claire, did you get my flowers?"

"You shouldn't have done that."

"But Claire, I want you to know how I feel about you."

"Please don't do anything like that again."

"But it was out of love, Claire. You must learn how to accept it. It's because you are stressed. I know you are stressed."

"Mehdi, I have to go."

"But Claire, just tell me yes to one thing. That we can have another class."

I am only an image in his head. As unreal as an actress on the screen. Soon his ardency will be focused on someone else. A customer in one of his shops, perhaps. Someone he meets on the street. She could be anyone, because she cannot be real. He can't imagine her growing old, falling ill, requiring all the forms of care that have nothing to do with his romantic fantasy.

"I have to go," I repeat.

I hang up.

I am almost at my client's door when my phone rings.

It's Destiny.

"Hi, Claire."

"Hi. What's going on?"

"Nothing. Just wondered how you were doing."

This is the first time Destiny has ever called simply to chat.

"Fine. You?"

"Okay. Doing okay."

But is she?

I hear something strained in her voice.

"I was wondering if you'd heard anything from that reporter," Destiny says.

"In terms of what?"

"She'd tell you if she found out some stuff about me, right?"

This is an odd question, and as she poses it, Destiny's tone becomes more urgent.

"Stuff about you?" I ask. "Like what?"

"You know, like about when I was on the street."

I feel Destiny's mind working. She is still worried about her talk with Julie Cooper. It's obvious that she's trying to escape a trap she thinks she's foolishly walked herself into. It strikes me that this is typical of her life, a tendency to charge ahead impulsively, then regret it and beat a swift retreat.

"Julie's not a cop, Destiny," I remind her.

"She's a writer, and the story she's writing isn't about what girls did while living on the street. It's about how they got off the street. How they made better lives. Which you've done, remember? Anything she wrote about you would be complimentary."

Destiny's anxiety appears to lessen somewhat. She switches to another subject.

"I've been thinking of that dead girl," she says. "I feel bad about her."

"Bad in what way?" I ask.

"Sorry for her. Because she, like, never talked. I mean . . . never."

When she doesn't elaborate, I try to draw her out.

"How often did you see her?" I ask.

"Just now and again. She'd show up on the beach. Paint. Then she'd just . . . disappear."

"She didn't sleep on the street?"

"I don't think so."

I ask a few more questions but fail to get more information out of Destiny. I sense that she's holding back, that this entire business of "feeling bad" for the girl at the pier is a screen for some deeper and less kindly motive for talking to me.

"If you know something more about this girl, you need to tell the police."

"The police?" Destiny yelps. "No way. Cops make stuff up. They might put it on me somehow."

"Put what on you?"

"What happened to her. Like maybe I had something to do with it."

This is preposterous. I want to dismiss it out of hand but stop myself, because Destiny's fear of being lied about, of no one believing her, is the same as my own.

I can't tell her that truth will win out in the end. Because there is no guarantee it will.

I can't assure her that innocence is enough. Because it isn't.

As I acknowledge the sheer bleakness of this truth, I realize that despite all the evidence to the contrary, I have harbored the absurd hope that something will protect Emma even if I don't.

Now I accept the awful fact that I alone stand in Simon's way.

He surely knows this, too.

My text pings as I'm headed home in the evening.

It's from Mehdi. One word: *Claire?*

The fact that he can reach me through the distance of digital space both disgusts and troubles me.

I delete his text.

Once at home, I can't stop thinking about my conversation with Destiny. It brings back the girl at the pier. I imagine her swimming toward me. I am the boat she is trying to reach. I watch helplessly as something pulls her beneath the waves. She surfaces, her white arms flaying in the air. Then she goes under again. This time she doesn't rise.

To restore some part of her life, I take the paintings Destiny gave me and place them wherever I can find space.

There are pictures of various landscapes. The mountains. The desert. The sea. Houses. These paintings are far more detailed than her drawing on the wall at Venice Beach. I see the shimmer of her nascent talent, her struggle to communicate her feelings, the eloquence of her untrained eyes.

A great wave of emotion sweeps through me. I'm carried away by it, picked up and brought down in the same eternal motion, like a body in the sea.

My mind plays its dirty trick. I see Melody. She looks to be around eighteen. She is standing in an artist's studio, shrouded in a white sheet.

A male voice: *Come to me.*

Melody walks across the room. The walls are hung with a great variety of paintings. She drifts past the Old Masters, then the Impressionists, the Expressionists. She is strolling through the history of art. At last she reaches a large metal tub filled with water. She lowers herself into it, still covered in the sheet. But it is wet now, and, wrapped in it, Melody is shivering.

Lower, the voice commands her.

I want to cry out. Plead with her not to sink further.

But she's beyond my call. She can't hear me. She does as she's told. Sinks further and further down until her face descends below the water, growing younger, the hair lightening, the features rearranging themselves until it is no longer Melody's face.

It is Emma's.

I must rescue her, but I know that any further contact with Simon will be useless.

That leaves only Charlotte.

SLOAN

I'D JUST SAT down to dinner when Miller called.

"It's Simon," he said. "And by the way, please call me by my first name."

"Okay."

"I just wanted to say thank you again for taking the time to watch those videos."

We talked a little longer. I told him that I'd made contact with Claire.

He was surprised.

"How did you manage that?" he asked.

"The tracking system got me within range of her," I explained. "After that, I looked around the area until I spotted her. When I did, I engaged her."

"Engaged?"

"I struck up a conversation with her. I found out that she's mentoring a girl off the street. That gave me an idea. I told her I was a reporter working on a story about girls who'd gotten off the street. She arranged for the three of us to meet, and after that Claire and I had a little chat."

"A little chat?"

From the tone of his voice, I couldn't determine whether Simon understood that by having a more intimate connection to Claire I could keep a closer eye on her, and perhaps even find a way to change her course.

"Friendly persuasion," I said, to make my strategy clearer. "I always try it first."

There was a pause before he asked, "How old is the girl? The one Claire's mentoring."

"She's a teenager."

"A teenager," Miller repeated thoughtfully. "That explains Claire's interest. She's trying to replace Melody."

When I offered nothing in response, Simon changed the subject. "Last night I did a little research on what happened to your father," he said. "The charges your mother made. They were very unfair."

"And never substantiated," I added quickly. "Because my mother took a quick exit."

"But her allegations were enough to stop your father from being commissioner," Miller said pointedly.

"Which is what she wanted."

"Of course, there's no real way to make it up to him now, but I was thinking that maybe something could be done to honor him. A scholarship in his name. What do you think?"

"I think he'd like that very much."

"Tell me about him."

I went through my father's long struggle, the odds against his success. I talked about his years in uniform, the torturous road he'd taken up the ranks to where commissioner of police had finally been within his grasp.

"Except for her," I said.

I thought of my mother, how utterly irresponsible she'd been, the evil accusations she'd made, the irreparable damage she'd done, the fact that she had denied my father the one job he'd worked for all his life.

"Someone should have stopped her before she destroyed your dad," Simon said.

"Yes," I agreed.

There was a pause before Simon added, "How will you stop Claire if 'friendly persuasion' doesn't work?"

"I'll go to Plan B."

"Which is?"

My answer was as dark as the trajectory of my mind at that critical moment. "Whatever it takes," I said.

CLAIRE

I KNOW I can't write to Charlotte, or email or text her.

She would not reply.

I can't call her on the phone either.

She wouldn't take the call.

Only one avenue is available to me.

Charlotte works at a jewelry store on Rodeo Drive. This is probably where Simon met her. I can easily recreate the scene: Simon gazing at a bracelet or a pair of earrings, asking which ones Charlotte admires. Later he will buy them for her. She will be amazed by his thoughtfulness, his memory. Simon is a master of this sort of thing. A magician at manipulation and deceit.

I have seen Charlotte only in the photograph that appeared with the announcement of her engagement to Simon. She is tall, slender, dressed elegantly. She will not be hard to recognize.

I arrive at the shop an hour before it opens and wait for her, half hidden by a marble column.

There is a surveillance camera at the entrance to the shop, along with others placed here and there along the corridor of high-end stores. Cameras have already recorded my approach, the way I have secreted myself, how I have stood and waited, waited, waited. I know how this can be seen by others.

Crazy Claire stalking Charlotte.

But I have no choice, since I don't know when her workday begins.

A few minutes later, I see her as she strides up the wide pedestrian boulevard. I expect her to go directly to work, but she veers to the right, where there is a pastry shop. Through its window, I watch as she sits down at a small table. She appears calm, almost pensive, sipping coffee.

I will never have a better opportunity.

All right, I tell myself. *Go.*

I move quickly toward the pastry shop, then down the narrow aisle to Charlotte's table.

She doesn't notice me until I sweep into the chair across from her.

She recognizes me instantly. Simon has obviously spoken of me, shown her my photograph, demonized me in every imaginable way. It doesn't surprise me that she immediately tenses, then reaches for her handbag.

"Please don't leave," I tell her.

Her gaze hardens. "What do you want?"

"Just to talk."

"I don't want to talk to you."

"A few minutes, that's all."

"I don't want to talk to you," she repeats stiffly.

"It's not about you marrying Simon. I'm not a jealous ex-wife. It's about Emma."

She is glaring at me now.

"I won't listen to this," she says icily.

I don't move.

Her eyes narrow menacingly.

"I'm leaving," she says evenly. "If you follow me, I'll call security."

"Please hear me out."

"No!" Charlotte says sharply.

She rises to her feet and stands peering down contemptuously.

"Never do this again," she warns.

"He's going after Emma. He did the same with my daughter. She warned me that he was—"

"Stop it!"

"I didn't believe her, Charlotte. She had nowhere to turn. So she got in a boat and the boat capsized and—"

"I don't want to hear this," Charlotte interrupts vehemently.

It is all pouring out of me now. The great burden of my guilt.

"By not believing her, I killed her. That's what I live with, Charlotte, and that's why, with Emma, I have to—"

She whirls around to leave, and as she does, I reflexively do something desperate. I grab her hand.

She yanks it from my grasp.

"How dare you touch me," she snaps, then rushes out of the pastry shop.

I can't help myself.

I go after her.

It is a scene of deranged pursuit, Charlotte dashing for the safety of her shop, me trailing behind her, calling after her.

"Charlotte, please."

When she makes it to the door of the shop, she wheels around.

"Not one more step," she says. "Or I'll call the police."

She stares at me brutally.

"And we both know what will happen to you after that."

I see myself in her eyes.

Claire out of control.

Claire with her paranoid delusions.

Dangerous Claire.

I want to break through this awful vision of me.

"Charlotte . . . one more word."

Her body is rigid.

Her gaze is stony.

I make my last effort to reach her.

"Believe your daughter."

2.

I'm gutted.

My body feels heavy. The air around me is thick and acrid. I am smoldering inside.

Then something rallies.

You cannot be undone by this, Claire, I tell myself, *You cannot give up.*

The phone rings just as I get to my car.

I shudder, convinced that it's Simon, that Charlotte has already told him. But it's a number I don't recognize.

"Hello?"

"Claire Fontaine?"

"Yes."

"This is Doctor Aliabadi. I'm calling from UCLA Hospital. Your father has been admitted here. I'm sorry to tell you, but he has had a heart attack."

I get as much information as I can from Dr. Aliabadi, then drive to the hospital.

My father is awake, but he only nods when I come through the door. He's very weak, half his energy drained from him. His white hair is disheveled, and his eyes open and close heavily, as if he is fighting sleep.

"I got this pain," he tells me.

His voice is shaky. There is a hint of astonishment in it. Some part of him cannot believe that his life from now on will be overshadowed by the prospect of his death.

"They say I had a heart attack."

He looks small, gaunt, as thin and frail as the aged musician in Picasso's *The Old Guitarist*, and with the same look of physical exhaustion.

"I thought I was going to die."

All his life he has been an angry man. Perhaps it was only Rose who could cool his wrath. Maybe that was why he'd wanted her so much, only to lose her when I made it to the boat.

My death had been his last hope for happiness. With what steaming ire he must over and over relive my unexpected survival.

A few minutes later he's asleep. I could go home, but I decide to stay.

It's hard to reconcile this dozing, weakened man with the athletic swimmer he once was, captain of his high school team.

I imagine him in his youth, churning through the glittering pool, a white wake behind him. Who was he then?

In books and movies, old foes forgive each other, put aside their grievances and make light of their ancient quarrels. Feuds are settled with a handshake, and everyone lives happily ever after.

There will be no such resolution with my father. He remains the man he has always been.

Selfish. Self-absorbed. Concerned only that his raging appetites be satisfied at any cost. At heart, a killer.

Rather than indulging some fantasy of settlement, I shift my focus to the old man who saved me. I remember his voice calling out to me: *Are you okay?* There are far more men like him than like my father.

I know that this is true.

Because if it weren't, the bodies of drowned daughters would roll in on every wave.

When I leave the hospital an hour later, I hear the *ting* of a message. Again I fear it is from Simon, infuriated by my confrontation with Charlotte.

It's Mehdi.

I have a present for you. I don't want to lose you, Claire.

How do you lose someone you never had?

But that isn't the end of his message. *You shouldn't treat me this way. You really shouldn't. It's not right to spit on me like this.*

Spit on him?

Obviously my failure to respond to Mehdi's romantic delusion has turned to grievance in him. Somehow he thinks that because he feels a certain way, I should feel that way, too.

But I don't.

In response, he is getting angry. I can hear it in

his text. The low rumble of a volcano. Still below the surface, but rising.

I look at the time.

I have only a few minutes to make it to my first client. I do my best, but I will be late. I call ahead to let her know.

The drive is about half an hour. On the way I try to return to the pleasure I'd felt when I talked with Ray, but less agreeable aspects of my life keep intruding.

First the smallest of them: Mehdi.

Then the big one: Simon.

My desperation spikes. It's like a fire inside me, sucking up the oxygen.

It is a huge relief when I reach my client's house and can step back into the open air.

"It's the first time you've ever been late, Claire," my client says when she opens the door. "Is everything okay?"

I catch myself in the mirror that hangs in the foyer. There is an explosive tension in my eyes. I have to pull back, calm myself. *All right, Claire, focus on your work.*

I look at Jennifer and smile my teacher's smile.

"Ready to get started?"

"Sure."

We walk onto her patio and take our seats at a wicker table.

Jennifer is a graduate student at UCLA in French history. She is in need of tutoring for her French language exam. At UCLA she will be given a page of text to translate into English, using only a French dictionary.

She has brought an excerpt from the historian Jules Michelet's history of the French Revolution. He writes a very formal French, less literary than, say, Marcel Proust, but challenging nonetheless. The page deals with the fountains of Versailles, along with the elaborate waterworks that made them possible and that were so noisy they kept the villagers of Marly from sleeping.

After we have read and translated together for a few minutes, Jennifer looks at me wonderingly. "Is Michelet saying that the noise of the waterworks at Marly was one of the causes of the French Revolution?"

"Yes, that's what he says."

"That's ridiculous, don't you think?"

"No. I can see his point."

She is clearly surprised by my answer. I try to explain.

"It's something that won't let you rest, that noise. Something that drives everything else from your head."

Jennifer is perplexed.

"A noise you can't get rid of," I tell her fiercely, almost angrily. "Like you can't get rid of guilt. Or rage. Or fear."

This outburst takes Jennifer aback.

"I see," she says.

I retreat to Michelet's text, but as the lesson goes on, I am continually dragged back into this struggle with Simon. His incessant noise!

My nerves are still jangling when I leave Jennifer. I need to quiet them, so I walk over to the small park across the street. A man is sitting on a bench. He is dressed in a dark blue suit. There is a large package beside him, beautifully wrapped and tied with an enormous ribbon.

Simon used to bring me flowers wrapped this way, boxed as a gift, with a lovely bow, but I can no longer imagine him as a suitor, nor myself as ever being the one he loved. Instead I conjure up another scene. The gift vanishes. The man is now Simon, but he is no longer alone. A second man sits beside him. They are discussing what can be done about me. They need a strategy to control me. They talk for a while, then they laugh. It's obvious that they have come up with the solution. A foolproof method to silence me. It will work perfectly, the conspiracy they've hatched. My fate now ticks forward intractably, like a well-timed watch. Best of all, whatever scheme they've dreamed up will be invisible. No matter what is done to me, it will appear that I did it to myself. All my wounds self-inflicted. No indication of a master plan. Ah, it is incredibly clever, their little plot. They rise and shake hands. How proud they are to have found a way to rid Simon of his problem.

My cell phone tings.

It's Nicolas, a trust-fund baby whose family fortune allows him to dabble in screenwriting. He is forty-four, and last summer he lived in Brussels, where he picked up a smattering of French. He has learned that France sometimes subsidizes films and wants to move there so he can market his work to the government. He thinks they are more likely to fund films about France and thus has decided to write about "the artists of Montmartre." The few pages of a script he has read to me suggest that he is more interested in drugs and sex than in artistic struggle.

I look at his message.

Gotta cancel, Claire.

A last-minute cancellation for which he offers neither apology nor excuse nor compensation.

I now have a two-hour interval between clients.

There is a coffee shop nearby. I go there, order an espresso, and take a seat by the window. A few tables away, a man is reading a travel magazine. A white sailing boat is on the cover. I know nothing about boats, but it looks very much like the one Simon rented in Catalina. I quickly turn away, because I don't want to be reminded of that night.

It's too late.

My memory unwinds like a film, absorbing in every detail. The boat rocking in the wind. The splatter of rain on the deck. The way Melody huddles beside the rail, peering out at the distant lights of the island.

I walk toward her. She turns to me, and I detect something disturbing in her eyes. I haven't noticed this before. I can't decipher it.

Melody, are you okay?

No, Mom, I'm not okay.

I close my eyes to shut out this memory.

Not long after she died, I happened upon a website called Tell Me Your Secret. The idea was to write postcards anonymously. You could pick the card you wanted. Some had flowers. Some had sunsets, landscapes, waterfalls. On these innocent-looking cards, you were to reveal a secret you could admit only to yourself. Some were innocuous: *I lie about my age.* Others more serious: *I don't love my husband anymore.* A few went dark: *I like hurting animals.* One was heartbreakingly raw: *When my sister lost her baby, I was glad.*

I remember staring at one of those blank postcards, my desire to expose my own unbearable secret so overpowering I could barely resist doing it, even anonymously.

But I did resist it.

I always have.

No one will ever know.

PART IV

SLOAN

ON THE PHONE, Simon's voice was taut. "She took the next step," he told me.

"What do you mean?"

"She confronted Charlotte."

"When?"

"Yesterday morning."

"Where? It couldn't have been at her house or I would have seen it on—"

"No, no. It was where she works. I should have given you that address, too."

Yes, he should have, I thought, but it was too late now.

"Charlotte didn't want to tell me. She knew it would upset me, but over dinner last night she broke down and just—"

"What happened?" I interrupted.

"Charlotte was just sitting in a pastry shop, waiting to go to work. Claire ran over to her and sat down at her table. Right across from her. When Charlotte tried to leave, Claire grabbed her hand. She physically accosted her! Charlotte pulled free and ran out into the street. Claire followed her. She practically chased her into the place where she works."

"I see."

What was done was done. Now what mattered was to make sure it didn't happen again.

"Are there any other places Charlotte goes that Claire might know about?"

"Just my house, of course. She comes there sometimes."

He seemed genuinely shaken by what Claire had done, and because he'd failed to mention Charlotte's workplace.

"What do we do now?" he asked.

His tone was very strained. He was at the end of his rope.

I thought fast and came up with a way to calm him down and buy time to devise a plan.

"Okay, it's time to play a harder game," I told him. "Let me do some digging."

"Digging for what?"

"Information on Claire," I answered. "Something I can use to come down on her."

This darker direction clearly appealed to Simon.

"Like a hammer," he said firmly. "No more Mr. Nice Guy. Because there's no predicting what she'll do next. Or to whom."

"I understand."

"Please keep in touch," Simon said. "I'm very concerned about where this is headed."

I promised him I would, then hung up and went to work.

When a case gets to such a flash point, sin eaters sometimes go nuclear. They're afraid they're going to fail their clients, and so they bring out the heavy artillery. I'd done the same from time to time, but I wasn't ready—not yet—to go that route with Claire.

It seemed better to defuse her.

One of my teachers in the police academy had once told the class that the human brain is designed to recognize a threat. Even when people are completely delusional, their primitive, reptile brains can detect any creature more dangerous than themselves.

His point was simple. The bottom line in people is fear. It can even trump madness.

When I applied this truth to Claire, the conclusion was obvious. She had to be threatened by something so deep it could penetrate her craziness, like an ice pick to her brain.

I started searching her file for anything that might force her into controlling herself. What could possibly do that? She wasn't intimidated by authority. She'd even attacked two fully armed police officers.

I went back through her records. If she'd been so much as given a ticket for speeding or written up for littering, I'd have found out about it. But aside from the psychotic break she'd had at Simon's house, her record was clean.

I thought I'd hit another dead end. But I didn't give up. There was another record, a case that might shine a harsh, exposing light on some dark corner in Claire Fontaine. I knew I wouldn't locate it under her name, however.

Fontaine, I typed into the LAPD databank search engine, *Melody.*

She came up under the usual headings: *Birth Certificate, Learner's Permit, US Passport.* Then things darkened: *Catalina Police Department, Catalina Island Medical Center, Catalina Island Mortuary.*

I called the cops on Catalina, told them I'd once been with the LAPD and was now working on what I called a case involving the death of Melody Slater. A Captain Patrino remembered the drowning. Yes, there'd been an investigation, but no charges had been filed. During the course of our conversation, he mentioned that Claire had been the last person to talk with Melody before she drowned.

I wondered if Claire had said something to her daughter that had compelled her to crawl into a dinghy and row away in a stormy sea.

I realized that this little tidbit of information wasn't much to go on, so I decided to check another source as well. It was a long shot, of course. There are lots of long shots in this business. The good news is that some of them pay off.

Candace Marks was sitting at her desk when I went into her office. "Sloan," she said brightly. "Good to see you."

She nodded toward the chair in front of her desk.

"Have a seat."

I sat down casually, as if there was nothing in particular on my mind.

"How are things in the catch-a-cop business?" I asked.

She laughed.

"Slow since the Rio Rancho bust."

Candace had been at the spearhead of a major LAPD scandal, an investigation into a drug-payoff scheme that had netted five retired cops and three that were still on duty. It had also garnered quite a few headlines for Candace herself.

She gave me one of her woman-to-woman winks. "Well, they don't call me 'Candy Cane' anymore. I'm the resident hard-ass now."

"Good for you."

She sat back in her chair, a gesture that made it clear that she was all business. "What can I do for you?"

"Claire Fontaine. Remember her?"

Candace shook her head.

"Simon Miller's wife."

"Oh, sure. The crazy one."

"That's right. Listen, I was just wondering if you'd talked to her at all. The day of the incident, I mean."

Candace shrugged. "Not that much. When

we got there, she'd already done a job on her husband's car."

As Candace went back through what Claire had done, I saw it all again. Claire with that paint, standing at the door, screaming at Candace and her partner before she hurled the can at them.

"She was yelling for us to back off," Candace told me. "To stay away from her. Then she threw a paint can at us. That's when we took her down."

"When she was in the squad car, did she say anything?"

"Yeah," Candace answered. "She said 'I'm sorry' a couple times."

"She was apologizing to you?"

Candace shook her head. "No, it didn't seem like it was to us." She shrugged. "I don't know who it was."

"Is that all she said?"

"Not another word, as far as I can recall."

I got to my feet and headed for the door. When I reached it, I turned to her. "Thanks."

Candace smiled. "All in the line of duty."

On the way back to my office, I went back over my conversation with Candace. From those thin pickings, I had only two words that might lead to something.

I'm sorry.

But to whom was Claire apologizing?

And for what?

CLAIRE

MY LAST SESSION ends at around five. Before going home, I look in on my father.

"He's sleeping," the nurse tells me. "He was having some problems. Dr. Aliabadi ordered a sedative."

"What kind of problems?"

"Anxiety."

"Is the doctor around?"

She is.

I meet with her in the office behind the nurses' station. She's around fifty, with close-cropped gray hair. She explains that my father became increasingly stressed during the day. This has caused a serious uptick in his blood pressure. "We're trying to stabilize it," Dr. Aliabadi explains.

"Do you know what caused the heart attack?"

"He has some constrictions in his arteries. It's not uncommon in older people, of course, but in your father's case, that's not the real problem."

"What is the real problem?"

"There's a lot of damage to his heart. If he has another cardiac incident, he almost certainly won't survive."

She waits for me to respond to this. When I don't, she says, "Do you have any questions?"

"No." I thank her and return to my father's room.

He is lying on his back, his hands on his chest. Like a man in a coffin. He was always good at playing any part his life required. I wonder if some reflexive part of him is acting even now.

I wait in the room a little longer, even though Dr. Aliabadi has made it clear that my father is down for the night. The little blip of his heartbeat moves raggedly across the screen of the monitor beside his bed. It beeps with the faded rhythm of his pulse. His life at last reduced to this mechanical movement. All that passion, frustration, and rage is now just the soft, ever-slowing syncopation of a departing life.

There is a terror in knowing how quickly a human future can be snatched away.

As Melody's was.

As Emma's yet may be.

I am thinking of Emma again, trying to decide what I should do next, when the door of my father's room suddenly opens.

A woman who looks to be in her early sixties takes two steps into the room, then freezes.

It is her large green eyes I recognize. They still seem young and passionate. The rest of her has gone the way of time, though she's clearly at war with the inevitable. Hair dyed black. There is an abundance of red lipstick. Her long eyelashes bat with surprise as she stares at me.

"Claire?"

She is obviously unsure if it's really me. I was very young when she last saw me. Only eight years old. My mature face is quite different from the one of my childhood. I might easily be a friend of my father's. Or even one of his care-givers.

"Rose," I say. "Hello."

She has not expected to run into me.

"Your father called me," she explains quickly. "Out of the blue. It was almost forty years ago that I worked for him."

She looks uncomfortable.

After all these years, she still must hide this old romance.

She glances toward my father, then back to me.

"He said he had a heart attack. Is he all right now?"

"There's a lot of damage, but he survived."

She is hesitant to go to him. Perhaps she thinks it would betray some glimmer of their affair.

"My husband died two years ago," she informs me.

She wants me to understand that whatever this is—my father's call, her response—it is not adultery.

I wonder if she knows about the boat. Did she plot it with him? Or was it something my father came to on his own?

"What did he say when he called you?"

"Just that he wanted to see me. To talk, I guess."

I try to imagine this conversation. Will they relive some torrid embrace?

A smile flickers onto her lips.

"Your dad was a great boss. A good father, too, as I'm sure you know."

What's the point of saying otherwise?

"How have you been?" I ask Rose.

"Fine."

She smiles briefly, then her expression changes into one I've never seen on her before. It's pity.

"I heard about your daughter. I'm very sorry. Such a tragedy."

I want to leave now.

"Well, make yourself comfortable," I tell Rose. "He may wake up soon. I'm sure he'll be pleased to see you."

I dash out of the room.

At home, I fall into a gloom of remembrance, Rose's pity ringing in my ears: *Such a tragedy.*

It is a relief when Ray arrives to look at the paintings. He gives me a bottle in a velvet gift bag. "Champagne."

I pour two glasses and hand one of them to Ray.

He notices the paintings spread about the room. "These are the ones you mentioned?"

"Yes."

He turns his attention to the largest of them. It's

a house, but with distortions. Some windows big, others small. Doors in odd places and leaning at unreal angles. It's quite different from the one the girl painted on the wall near McDuffy's, though there is the same misshapenness and disorder.

"It's a broken home," he says.

He goes on to the next painting.

"What do you think?" he asks.

It's a forest. A very tangled one, shrouded with vines that sprout enormous leaves. Jungle lushness, a suffocating quality in its density. A landscape strangling itself.

When I tell Ray all this, he stares at me very closely.

"That's a very dark interpretation, Claire."

"Yes, well, a teacher of mine once said that when we look at a painting, we repaint it with the colors and shapes that are inside us." I take a sip from my glass. "What do you see?"

"Confusion. Lostness."

Ray proceeds to the next painting, a swirl of colors above what appears to be a storm-tossed sea, though it might also be a field of wheat.

"There's a lot of movement," he says. "Things rising and falling. It almost breathes."

He considers it a while longer, then goes to the next two, another house, equally surreal, and a seascape in which the water seems to be reaching hungrily for the beach.

"I'm looking for a theme. Something that can tie them all together for an exhibit."

His gaze drifts from one painting to the next. "Do you see anything that connects them?"

"Not really."

Ray continues to concentrate on the paintings.

"Let's just call the exhibit 'Her World.' Then people can make whatever connections they like."

"Don't they do that anyway?"

He looks at me and smiles.

"At least it's a way of not forgetting her."

There is kindness in his voice and in his eyes.

"Or the way she saw the world," he adds.

I realize just how much I am drawn to this man.

At the same time I must keep my distance, and make Ray keep his.

2.

I am still in the midst of this feeling when I meet Ava for lunch the next day.

She has chosen a new place for us to have lunch, the A.O.C. on Third Street. It specializes in tapas.

"Little bites are great. You can eat the whole menu."

She watches as I survey the choices.

"You look . . . different."

"Do I?"

She studies me a moment. "Could it be something to do with Ray Patrick?"

"He came over last night. We had a nice talk."

The waiter appears. We order a selection of tapas and as always I have my sparkling wine.

"A nice talk? Forgive me, but it looks like more than that."

"What do you mean?"

"That glow, Claire. When I see it, I get the idea that someone's met Mr. Right. Or at least thinks she might have. Which is it with you?"

If I tell her about Ray's coming to see the paintings, she will lecture me about my unfortunate tendency to bring up "dark things." She will remind me that this is a new relationship that should not be burdened with such depressing issues. She will tell me to keep things light, upbeat, casual.

"Ray and I just talked," I tell her. "Like friends."

"Oh, please."

"It's true."

"Are you telling me that you just want to be friends with Ray?"

"It wouldn't matter anyway, Ava. I have to get my life in order before I can have a relationship."

Ava's mood darkens.

"Meaning?" she asks.

"Meaning I can't get involved with anyone until I've cleared away the rubble."

"And the rubble is Simon, of course. He's a big pile, I know. The trick is to ignore him."

"Or kill him."

Something in the tone of my voice, or the look in my eyes, stuns Ava. She quickly adds a warning.

"That's how it starts, Claire. You begin with something you couldn't possibly do. And then the more you think about it, the more it seems not only possible but a pretty damn good idea. It's a dangerous train of thought."

Dangerous, yes.

Because I find myself imagining a world without Simon. One in which he can do no further harm. I don't consider guns, knives, or some blunt instrument. Rather, I dream of him disappearing into the depths, like a body thrown overboard.

Sinking.

How much better life would be if men like Simon littered the bottom of the sea.

3.

I arrive at Margot's apartment at just after two in the afternoon. She's a new client, and from the sound of her voice, I expect to see a woman in her forties.

But a man opens the door. He's powerfully built. A wrestler's body. Muscular thighs and bulging biceps.

"I'm Claire."

The look he gives me is as familiar as it is uncomfortable. A gaze that unzips and unbuttons and leaves your clothes on the floor. His eyes crawl across my chest.

"The French teacher."

He steps back to let me in.

"Margot will be out in a minute."

I walk into the house.

"I was just on my way out."

But he doesn't leave. He directs me into the living room and trails behind me. The heat of his eyes is on my hair, my shoulders, my waist, then down and down.

"I'm a fireman," he tells me with a slight smile.

Obviously I should be impressed.

"Beverly Hills. Over on North Rexford. We get the movie-star calls. Mansions. But fire is fire.

It doesn't make exceptions." He waits for me to respond. When I don't, he adds, "Where do you live?"

"Near the Grove."

"Station Sixty-One," he says in a bragging tone. "On Third Street. I know some of those guys."

He is clearly about to continue along these lines when Margot enters the room. Her appearance irritates him, as if she is a heckler in the audience, spoiling his act.

He looks at her.

"I'll be home late," he tells her.

He turns to me.

"I'm Matt, by the way. I'm sure we'll meet again."

He gives me a quick smile, then heads for the door.

Margot's posture relaxes when he goes through it.

"We can work here," she says. She means the small table across the room.

"Sure, fine."

Margot was born in the Drôme, in the southeast of France. She was five years old when her parents were killed in a car accident. Her father was American, and she was taken in by his parents. Her grandparents did not speak French, so she has spoken English most of her life. She has retained a surprising amount of her childhood French, however. Her vocabulary is basic, but even the little French she knows touches her emotionally.

"It's like going home. Being with my parents again."

As we go through the lesson, it's clear that Margot is very bright. For some of my students, an hour of French can be exhausting. But Margot thrives on it. She comes alive with each new word.

"I can't wait for the next lesson," she says as I am leaving.

"I can't either."

She is still at her door when I reach my car. "*Au revoir*," she calls. "*Merci beaucoup*."

"*De rien*. You're welcome."

Dominic is my final client of the day.

I always dread my time with him.

There is a disturbing element in everything he does. His eyes seem never to meet mine, and when he speaks, it is little more than a sulking mutter.

We begin with common verbs, but as always he veers the lesson toward the faintly criminal. Today he asks for the French verb for "to kidnap."

"Why that word?" I ask him.

"It's in the game. The one I play in my room."

"A game about kidnapping?"

He nods.

"You try to get away with it," he says. "The cops are after you. The FBI. You have to do the kidnapping, pick up the ransom, and get away with it."

"Who do you kidnap?"

He grins.

"A girl."

This game clearly provides him with a disturbing excitement. "After I get the ransom," he says in a tone of perverse empowerment, "it's up to me to decide what to do with her."

"You don't have to let the girl go?"

He shakes his head. "Not if I want to keep her."

I look at him sternly, not at all sympathetic to this horrid game.

"Why would you keep her, Dominic?"

The question closes him down.

He returns his gaze to the textbook.

"It's just a game," he says sullenly, with a hint of resentment that he's been drawn into an uncomfortable interrogation.

I continue the class without giving him the French infinitive for "kidnap," which happens to be exactly the same, *kidnapper.*

We practice vocabulary and work through a few present-tense conjugations.

I keep my eye on the clock, because I don't want to spend a single extra second with Dominic.

When the class ends, he remains at the desk

while I gather up my stuff and head for the door.

On the way I pass his room. The door is open. I can see his computer screen. The game's logo is glowing in the darkness inside the room. Two leering eyes, and the sinister title: *Watchman.*

I whirl around.

Dominic is still at the desk, staring at me with a *gotcha* glimmer in his eyes that confirms what he's done as well as the sick pleasure he takes in it.

Suddenly I am on fire.

I storm down the corridor.

"I know what you did," I say to him coldly.

Dominic laughs.

"It was just a joke."

"A joke?" I demand vehemently. "You think it's funny to play with someone? To threaten someone?"

My voice echoes through the house.

"Do you?"

He faces me mutely.

"Do you?"

"What's going on?"

I turn to see Dominic's mother staring at me in utter consternation.

"What's going on here?" she repeats.

"Your son is a—"

She cuts me off.

"I think you'd better leave, Miss Fontaine."

I want to tell her about the Watchman, the

message, but she'll dismiss it as a prank. I have no choice but to leave.

At the door, I look back.

Dominic is staring at me with the Watchman's leering eyes.

My nerves are still jangling when I reach home.

I am filled with self-doubt.

Can I no longer trust myself at all?

First I was wrong about Mehdi's flowers, and now I have been wrong about the email from the Watchman.

Simon had nothing to do with either of these things. Even when he does nothing, he baits me.

I glance about the room. My books. My music. None of it calms me.

I hear an alert. The tone tells me that I've just gotten a review on Yelp.

All my reviews have been positive. I check this one in the hope of finding a few kind words. I open the app and read:

Be warned. This woman is mentally unstable. She should not be allowed in your home. She is dangerous.

Dominic!

Or his mother!

Ting.

The same devastating review on Thumbtack.

Another *ting.*

Craigslist.

They are trying to destroy me.

I feel completely shattered.

I need to talk to someone.

Normally I would call Ava, but our last exchange was less pleasant than usual. I don't feel like going to her.

Only one person comes to mind.

I am wary of making the call.

After all, we hardly know each other.

I think of the last time I saw him, my determination to keep my distance. That caution has dissolved in the wake of these hateful reviews.

I pick up my phone, tap out the number, and wait.

"Ray?" I say when he answers.

"Yes."

"Ray . . . I . . ."

"What's the matter?"

"I . . . I . . ." My voice breaks. I can't go on.

"I'll be right over," Ray tells me.

He arrives a few minutes later.

"What happened?" he asks as I usher him into the house.

I tell him about Dominic, about the flowers from Mehdi, even about the Yelp review.

He listens carefully as the two of us sit in the living room of my house.

My voice is steady, but my nerves are clanging.

I know I sound as if I'm overreacting, and for

that reason I have no idea how he may respond to the odd things I'm telling him.

When I'm done, he remains quiet for a brief interval before he asks, "You didn't think it was any of those people who did these things, right? You thought it was someone else?"

"Yes."

"Who?"

I've gone as far as I'd intended to go in my story. "I don't want to say more," I answer.

Ray looks at me strangely. "Why not?"

"Because you may think I'm crazy."

He smiles. "You don't seem crazy to me."

He looks at me determinedly.

"Who, Claire?"

I hesitate, though I know the time has come.

"Simon," I answer. "Simon Miller."

Ray obviously recognizes the name.

"We were married for five years," I add.

He doesn't ask any more questions.

I know I can stop now. I don't have to reveal anything more about myself. That's when I know that the author I read so long ago was right.

The essence of falling in love really is jeopardy.

And so I take a chance.

"Simon is . . . a very bad man," I begin.

Then I tell him everything.

SLOAN

I CONTINUED TO believe that the best way to free Simon of Claire's accusations was for Claire to relent. She had to recognize the damage she was doing. Or had already done.

At some point while thinking this through, I remembered the one time my father had stopped my mother in her tracks. Before then, he'd taken her behavior in his stride. But suddenly he'd wheeled around, glared at her coldly, and said, "If you're such a great mother, where's Layla?"

Layla.

The child she'd had before meeting my father, a little girl she'd simply dropped off at her grand-mother's house in Memphis and never seen again.

At the mention of Layla, my mother had gone completely silent, then turned away and headed into the bedroom, where she'd stayed until morning.

What had been my father's single effective weapon against her?

Shame.

I wondered if the same tactic might work with Claire as well.

To answer that question, I needed to know more about her.

Private stuff I could use to get her off Miller's back.

I'd interviewed Simon Miller, watched his video, searched the public records, read the police reports, talked to Candace. I'd combed the Internet in search of some key to Claire. I'd found nothing of importance.

Other than Claire herself, I had only one source of information left: Destiny. I waited until around ten o'clock before I called her.

"Twenty-four seven," a man's voice answered.

"Is Destiny there?" I asked.

I heard the man call her to the phone.

"Coming," she shouted back.

She sounded stressed out, wound tight.

"I'm beat," she said to someone as she took the phone, "It's Destiny, who's this?"

"It's Julie Cooper."

Destiny instantly went on guard.

"Oh," she said cautiously. "Hi."

I added a touch of urgency to my approach.

"I think we should talk again."

"What about?"

I heard worry in her voice, and worked it with a vague bluff.

"I think you know."

The silence at the other end of the line told me that Destiny had something to hide. I remembered the strained look in her face when I'd mentioned Vicki Page, so I opened that door first.

"Vicki," I said. "Vicki Page."

Destiny's voice went dark. "I can't talk about her."

The change of tone told me that she'd had more than a casual relationship with Vicki.

I used the old ploy of suggesting that the snitch had been snitched on. "What if I were to tell you that she's talking about you?" I asked.

"To who?"

When I didn't answer, there was a tense pause before she added, "To the cops?"

I waited.

"Are you a cop?" Destiny asked.

"No, I'm not."

"So why do you want to know about Vicki?"

"Let's just say I'm looking to corroborate her story."

"Vicki's story . . . about me?"

Silence did the trick again.

"Vicki gave me up?" Destiny asked.

Once again I held fire.

"She gave you stuff about me?"

Destiny's questions told me all I needed to know: Destiny had done something for which she could be ratted on by Vicki Page. In her mind, Vicki had already thrown her under the bus. Now she could do the same to Vicki. Such was life in the marginal world they both inhabited. No one was ever more important than yourself. You'd be a fool to think any other way. A philosophy of life sin eaters easily leverage to their advantage.

Which was exactly what I intended to do.

"When's your next break?" I asked.

"Three o'clock."

"I'll be waiting in the parking lot. Look for a dark blue Maxima."

"Okay," Destiny said. "But you got to promise me you're not a cop."

"I told you that."

"Yeah . . . but."

"Destiny, if I were a cop, I'd tell you."

"Okay," Destiny said. "We can talk."

I knew she was already trying to figure out exactly what Vicki Page had told me. More important, she was working on how to get herself out of the fix she was in. Making a list of the people she'd be willing to betray.

There was only one name I wanted to be on it.

Claire Fontaine.

Five hours later, Destiny walked toward my car. She looked smaller and more vulnerable than before, like a boxer facing an opponent twice her size. The only question in her mind was how quickly she could end the fight and crawl out of the ring.

"Hi," she said weakly as she got into my car.

I went straight to the point.

"Destiny, you need to come clean," I told

her in a voice I made as sisterly as possible.

Destiny looked at me as if my opinion of her mattered more than that of anyone she'd ever known.

"I'm not a bad person," she said meekly. "I'm really not."

"I know you're not. But I have to trust my sources, Destiny. Their background. What they've done. Make sure they're reliable. I don't want anything to pop up that I should have known about. I'm sure you understand."

"Okay," Destiny murmured.

She was primed to answer any question I might ask. I started probing.

"You worked for Vicki Page, correct?"

She nodded halfheartedly.

"Not for long, though," she said. "And I was never one of her girls. I just helped her out a little."

"What did you do?"

She looked at me hesitantly.

"You won't tell the cops, will you?"

"No."

"Or Claire?"

"I won't tell anyone," I assured her. "This is strictly off the record. Otherwise I'd be taking notes on our conversation. And as you can see, I'm not doing that."

She smiled slightly. "Yeah, sure. You have to trust your sources."

She sounded like a journalist well aware of the rules of her profession.

I took this occasion of imagined collegiality to press ahead.

"If you weren't one of Vicki's girls, what did you do for her?"

"I introduced her to other girls."

I played a hunch and raised the stakes. "Was the girl off the pier one of them?"

"Yes."

This question put Destiny on edge. She needed a little breathing space. I gave it by changing direction.

"What's in your background, Destiny? Anything . . . criminal?"

"Nothing much. Okay, arrested a couple of times, but not bad stuff."

She made this seem like a blameless life.

"It's not like I killed somebody or something," she added.

I didn't care about her past offenses. Asking about them was just a way of luring her toward me, making her feel I was her confidante.

"No, not bad at all," I said lightly.

She smiled.

I acted as if that's all I'd come for and I was now satisfied that Destiny was a "reliable source."

"Thanks for being honest with me," I added in a way designed to make her think that I now trusted her completely.

She immediately relaxed. "That's it?"

"Yeah," I said.

I offered her Julie Cooper's big bright smile.

"That wasn't hard, was it?" I asked cheerfully.

"I guess not," Destiny answered.

We chatted about her workday for a few minutes. I let her complain about her job before circling back to Vicki. She was off her guard now because she thought I'd already gotten what I'd come for. Circling back wouldn't bother her at all. She probably wouldn't even notice.

"By the way," I began casually, "what made you think the girl on the pier would be good for Vicki?"

I made it sound like procuring a girl for Vicki Page was no more serious than choosing a kitten for a friend.

"I told her she was young and pretty and that she never talked, that I'd never heard her say a word. Vicki said, 'Yeah, good, guys like that type.'"

"Vicki thought she was . . . good material?"

"Yeah."

"Then what?"

"She set it up."

"What does that mean?"

"She set it up for me to bring the girl to her. So she could take a look at her."

"Where did you take her?"

"Vicki's house. I sort of made friends with the

girl. I told her I had another friend. Someone she'd probably like."

"What happened then?"

"I took her to Vicki's place. Once we got there, Vicki gave her some pie. Apple pie, I think. Then she took her into another room. When they came out again, the girl didn't know much of anything."

"Why not?"

"Because Vicki shot her up."

"Drugged her?"

"Yeah. She did it before we left LA. By the time we got to this other place, the girl was out of it."

An older part of me suddenly kicked in. The part that had once been a cop.

I suddenly remembered that on the day I started at the academy, my father told me a story about how when Satan was booted out of heaven, he had fallen and fallen. But a feather had dropped from him before he went over the edge of Paradise, and this one part of him remained in heaven. "Even if you fall, Sloan," he said to me, "always remember that feather, and try to get back to it."

"Where is this other place?" I asked.

"Out in the desert somewhere. The middle of nowhere. It took us about an hour to get there. Maybe more."

"What happened when you got to this house?"

"We waited in the car. The girl was in the back seat. Out of it. That's the way some of Vicki's customers like to have them. Knocked out. So they don't remember them."

"What happened next?"

"Vicki's customers showed up. She took the girl inside. About an hour later she brought the girl back to the car. She was still out of it. We took her back to Venice Beach. The next thing I heard she was in the water."

"How long after she was with Vicki did she end up dead?"

"Not long. A few days."

She shrugged.

"She was a one-shot wonder, that girl. That's what Vicki called her."

I wasn't sure how much of Destiny's story was true. I probed it here and there, looking for holes, but she stuck to her tale. I could have grilled her for another hour, but what would have been the point? Even the parts she'd made up would have hardened in her mind.

I had one more trick to play.

"The problem is the girl they found off the pier looks very young," I said, as if my sympathies were entirely with Destiny. "Early teens, probably."

Destiny was now wary, but she kept quiet.

"That would make you a child-sex trafficker," I added in a tone that made it clear I was really sorry that Destiny had gotten herself into such a serious situation. "You'd be looking at twenty years."

I made it sound as if I found this quite unjust, given that Destiny had fallen into this trap.

"Twenty years?" Destiny asked. "Just for . . . I mean, I didn't . . ."

"I know," I told her. "It's Vicki who should take the rap. Unfortunately, you're in it, too."

She was trapped now.

The moment had come to seal the deal.

"Maybe I can help you," I said.

For effect, I let a beat go by before I added, "Because I'm not a writer."

Destiny's eyes flashed. "You're a cop! I knew it!"

"I was a cop at one time," I admitted. "But not anymore."

Destiny stared at me uncomprehendingly.

"I'm what they call a sin eater, a fixer. I help people out of the difficult situations they get themselves into."

Destiny remained bewildered. She knew the game had changed, but she didn't know in what way.

"Do you and Claire share things?" I asked. "You know what I mean. You tell her a secret. She tells you a secret. That sort of thing."

Destiny's eyes widened in stunned recognition.

"Are you helping somebody with Claire?" she asked.

"It's better if you don't ask too many questions," I said. "It's safer just to answer mine."

I waited a beat, then repeated the question.

"Do you and Claire share things about your lives?" I asked emphatically. "Details. Intimacies."

I looked her dead in the eye. "Yes or no?"

"Yeah. It's supposed to help us get close. Sharing stuff."

"Does Claire ever talk about her daughter?"

"Yeah, she's talked about her. She drowned. She feels guilty about it."

"Why does she feel guilty?"

"Because they had words the night she drowned."

"Did she tell you any of these words?"

"Just that they were bad," Destiny answered. "And Claire never got to take them back or say she was sorry."

I remained silent, and during that interval I saw that Destiny had picked up the scent and was now enjoying herself.

"A sin eater," she said, almost excitedly. "Wow."

She was clearly intrigued by the unexpected turn her story had taken. She looked like a girl who'd just seen the first episode of a show she really liked and was impatient for the next one.

"I could help you," she added. "With Claire, I mean. Whatever you need to find out. Like your partner, you know? Your sidekick."

Her eyes had a malignant sparkle.

"I can get her to talk. I know I can. What do you want to know?"

There was a delicious relish in her manner. Life was just a dirty game to Destiny, and it didn't matter how you won.

"Really," she told me assuredly. "I know how to make her talk."

When I looked at her doubtfully, she took it as a challenge and reached for her phone.

"I'll prove it to you," she said almost gleefully.

She tapped the speakerphone.

"Listen," she said, then dialed Claire's number.

Claire picked up immediately. "Hi," she said.

Destiny winked at me.

"It's Destiny," she said in a voice that made her sound broken and in need of help. "I'm not having a good day, Claire."

"What's happening?" Claire asked.

"Everything. It's like everything is against me. Ganging up, you know? And there's no way out." She added a tremble to her voice. "Except to just ditch it all. Like, why bother?" She acted as if she were fighting back tears. "I've been trying, Claire. I've been trying to do better. Stay off drugs. Keep my job. But it's hard when you're all alone, you know?"

Claire sounded worried.

"Destiny, where are you?"

"It doesn't matter. Nothing matters."

"No, Destiny," Claire said urgently. "Don't think that way."

"I can't help it, Claire."

"Are you at home? I'll be right there."

"No, no," Destiny blurted. "I'm at work. I'll go home at the end of my shift."

"When does your shift end?"

"At six."

"Okay, I'll meet you at your apartment," Claire said.

"You don't have to do that. I'm not worth it."

Destiny's tone took on the confused desperation of a lost child.

"You're all I have, Claire," she said.

When she hung up, she looked at me and smiled.

"Claire's in the palm of my hand now," she said.

She pocketed her phone with a self-satisfied flourish.

"She'll be all warm and fuzzy when I see her," she added proudly.

She was grinning happily, pleased with having manipulated Claire so easily.

"She'll open up to me."

She was confident she'd escaped another trap.

"What do you want to know?" she asked.

"Have her talk about her last conversation with Melody on the boat."

"Okay," Destiny said breezily. "No problem."

When I added nothing, she said, "You want to, like, give me your card or something?"

"What for?"

"So I can call you after this meet-up with Claire. I mean, we should keep each other posted, right?"

"Don't worry, I'll keep in touch."

She seemed to think that we were now on an equal footing. Two professional sin eaters.

"Maybe I could work for you," she said. "It seems like fun."

I let her believe this.

"And I'd be good at it," Destiny added enthusiastically.

It struck me that the world inside Destiny's head was entirely unreal. One in which procuring an underage girl led quite naturally to an upward career move.

I kept these thoughts to myself, of course.

"Let's see how well you do with Claire," I told her.

She seemed almost to melt in the warm glow of a new career possibility. "This could be great."

I smiled.

"Yes," I said. "It could."

CLAIRE

DESTINY OPENS THE door, then steps back to let me in.

Her apartment looks more like a place hastily abandoned than where someone actually lives. Clothes are strewn about, as well as take-out boxes from 24/7. The sofa bed is pulled out, the bedding wadded up, with part of a blanket pouring over the side, where it gathers in a ratty pool on the floor.

"Just a second," Destiny says as she clears a space on one of the studio's two chairs. When she finishes, she shrugs. "Okay, I'm not a neatnik."

She seems to feel that the untidiness of her apartment reflects the disarray in her life. Which it may. But I'm not here to judge. I sit down and wait for Destiny to speak. She has brought me here to listen. That's what I intend to do.

"I eat takeout," she says. "Otherwise I'd offer you something."

"That's okay."

Destiny pauses briefly, then begins. "Everything sucks."

She reaches for a pack of cigarettes, thumps one out, and offers it to me.

"No, thanks."

She takes the cigarette and lights it.

"I know I have to shake off this mood. Because it'll only get worse if I don't, right? And I do want to tell you everything, Claire. I really do. But maybe not just now. I'm sick of talking about my screwed-up life."

Her gaze darts about the room as if she's looking for a subject among the clutter. Finally she settles it on me.

"How about you?" she asks. "Let's talk about your life instead of mine."

She sucks violently at the cigarette, then fires a line of smoke into the smelly air.

"Christ, this place is a dump," she says contemptuously. "I live in a dump."

She shifts edgily in her chair.

"What a wreck I am."

She looks at me plaintively.

"I bet your daughter wasn't like me. A mess like I am. I bet she was great. You never told me much about her."

"What do you want to know?"

"Well, like, how old was she?"

"Fifteen."

"I'm sorry about what happened to her, Claire."

Silence is my only response.

"I wish I'd had a mother like you. I remember the last time I saw my mom. She was yelling at me, 'I wish you'd never been born.' "

She lowers her head and starts to cry.

I let her weep.

When she regains control of herself, she looks up at me, and through her tears she says, "Talk to me about Melody. About you and her."

"We had some issues," I tell her. "We argued. That's what hurts the most. The fact that our last conversation was an argument."

"About what?"

For the first time since I've known her, Destiny appears truly interested in something other than herself.

"About what, Claire?"

SLOAN

IT WAS JUST after eight in the evening when Destiny called me. She'd had her meeting with Claire. She had things to tell me.

"Go ahead."

"Not over the phone."

"Why not?"

"Somebody might hear."

I couldn't tell if she actually suspected that my phone was bugged or if she was merely into the drama of the situation.

"I'll meet you at our usual spot," she said.

I didn't feel like arguing the point. We settled on a time, and I headed back to 24/7.

Destiny was standing in the shadows at the far end of the lot, smoking. When she saw me, she tossed away her cigarette and came toward my car briskly, with a bouncy step.

"Hey," she said breezily when she got in.

"How did it go?"

"Good," Destiny said happily. She looked like an agent who'd just returned from a successful mission. She was obviously eager to give me her favorable report.

She'd spent nearly two hours with Claire. During that time she'd done her poor-little-runaway routine. It had worked like a charm, she told me. Claire had been totally sympathetic. All ears to whatever story popped into Destiny's mind. In the end, however, she'd managed to direct the conversation to Claire's life.

"She got real sad at that point," she said in the confident tone of a seasoned informer. "She told me that she and Melody had been having some trouble. Melody was moody. She started staying in her room. Claire figured it was just puberty. Like girls get. Quiet. Withdrawn. That's the way it was with Melody."

Destiny was in full swing now, stringing out small details in a dramatically conspiratorial tone. She might have been revealing the secrets to the A-bomb.

At last we arrived at the boat.

"That's why they went on that sailing vacation. They could all be together. Relax. All of them on her husband's boat."

Her eyes shimmered with pleasure. She was reveling in her new role as spy and informer.

"Something happened on that boat," she said darkly, like a character in a melodrama. "Between Claire and Melody. And it must have been bad, because that's when Melody decided to leave. Even in that stormy weather."

"Did Claire tell you what happened between them?"

"No. That's where she went quiet. Like it hurt too much. Or maybe she couldn't deal with it.

Anyway, I got the feeling things came to a head between them that night on the boat. Claire didn't say what the deal was, but I got to thinking, and something came to me."

She smiled confidently, with an air of pride that she'd gotten the goods. "Melody was fifteen, right? Looking more . . . grown-up. I know what it's like to have this . . . power. You can drive a guy crazy flashing it around. Especially an old guy."

"An old guy?"

"Yeah. Like Claire's husband."

"What are you getting at?"

"That maybe Claire felt threatened."

"By Melody?"

"Yes."

Destiny could hardly contain how clever she thought she was.

"It would be scary, right?" she asked excitedly. "Having this hot young girl traipsing around while you're getting old."

She watched me closely, making sure that I was getting the full implications of her story.

"What I'm saying is that maybe Claire resented Melody. Thought she was stealing her husband, showing off the goods like that."

She paused before revealing a theory she considered pure genius.

"It could even be a motive."

"A motive for what?"

"For Claire to kill her."

I gave Destiny no hint that I didn't find her theory remotely plausible. I let her believe that I might actually see Claire and Melody's last conversation as she did.

With Claire seized by jealousy. Resentful of Melody. Harsh, angry words.

Then, at some point, Claire murders Melody. It was a ridiculous B-movie scenario that didn't fit with the facts of Melody's death, but I allowed Destiny to entertain the illusion that she'd actually solved the case.

"I found it, didn't I?" she asked excitedly. "The truth about Claire."

She thinks we're partners, I told myself.

Which I suppose we were, since she would be my way into Claire, the hammer I could use to crush her.

Though the cop in me, that small spot where the badge still faintly glowed, insisted, against all evidence, that we were not.

CLAIRE

I GET HOME just after eight. Unlighted, the house seems lonelier, and there is a faintly frightening aspect to the darkness that surrounds it.

I feel a spike of fear as I get out of my car and head toward the front door. To control it, I repeat the usual assurances.

No one is crouched behind a bush.

No hired thug is waiting in the shadowy foyer.

There are no footsteps rushing at me from behind.

Once inside, I turn on the lights. The house is just as I left it.

Nothing has moved. Nothing is out of place.

And yet I can't tamp down my anxiety that my most private space has been invaded.

I sit down on the sofa and work to calm my vibrating nerves. I close my eyes and try to think of something good.

Ray comes to mind. Our last meeting. How lovely it was. I try to let that memory drive back my darker thoughts. I close my eyes and let the warmth of that evening settle over me.

I see his face and hear his voice, and they seem so real that when the doorbell rings, I hope that it's Ray, walk to the door, and open it.

"Claire," he says when I open the door.

I am startled. "Mehdi."

"I have been waiting for you."

He is holding a small blue box.

"For you, Claire. Because I forgive you."

"Forgive me for what?"

"For him. For the one who comes here all the time."

A chill passes over me. The notion of Mehdi parked near my house, watching it from behind the wheel, is unnerving.

"I have a gift for you."

He presses the blue Tiffany box toward me.

"Please. It is for you. Very expensive, Claire."

I shake my head, refusing it.

"I don't take presents from clients, Mehdi," I tell him firmly. "I think you should leave now."

To my astonishment, he says, "No, I come in. We talk. You know I love you."

When I start to close the door, he reaches up and presses his hand against it.

"You lied to me, Claire."

He pockets the box.

"Maybe you don't deserve my gift."

"I want you to leave, Mehdi."

"Just a little time, Claire."

He looks at me hungrily.

"Thirty minutes."

He draws in a trembling breath.

"With your body."

I glare at him, stricken, speechless.

"Give me thirty minutes. Only thirty minutes, Claire. I will forgive you, and you take my gift, eh?"

His demand is utterly repulsive.

"We kiss first, okay? Then I start the clock, yes? After kiss."

I try again to close the door, but his hand forces it back.

Then Mehdi lunges forward, and I am abruptly crushed in his arms. He presses his mouth against my tightly closed lips, moving his head in a sideways sawing motion as if he is trying to fuse our mouths together. I try to pull back, but he yanks me toward him more forcefully. I can feel the flick of his insistent tongue, like the head of a snake burrowing between my lips.

I jerk my head back violently.

"Stop it!"

He steps back.

"Okay, I stop."

He peers at me as if he has just been crowned the prince of Persia. There is a smirk on his lips.

"I got what I needed from you."

He waves the box in my face.

"I can return it."

He regards me almost dismissively.

I am a piece of meat he has chewed as much as he likes and can now spit out.

"I don't need Claire," he says. "I'm over her."

249

He turns and walks away with a triumphant little prance.

I stand at the door, shaking with rage.

I want to run after him, tackle him, beat him to death. But I only stand and scowl at him as he strides toward his car.

When he reaches it, he turns back toward me, raises his arm victoriously, and pumps the air, as if signaling his triumph to a city he has conquered.

I turn back toward my door, but I can't go in.

A foul air has entered it, the smell of Mehdi's cologne.

I need a cleansing sea breeze.

I get in my car, roll down the windows, and head toward the ocean.

I want the rushing wind in the car to blow away every trace of Mehdi.

Not just his smell, but also the foul taste of his mouth, his lips, his reptilian tongue.

I hardly know how far I've gone when I realize that I am on Melrose.

Ray's gallery.

He may be there.

I want to see him.

I press the accelerator and speed ahead, moving toward him as fast as I can.

The lights are on in the gallery, and as I go up the stairs I see Ray standing toward the back. He isn't facing me, but I know it's him, and a huge relief washes over me.

I open the door and head toward the back of the gallery.

Ray is talking to someone I cannot see.

I hear his voice distantly at first, then more clearly as I come nearer.

A few feet away, I stop and listen.

A teenage girl stares at him adoringly, no doubt impressed by his command of the subject.

He is talking to her about a painting, locating its stylistic touches in the history of art.

His tone is thoughtful, persuasive.

He is speaking with great authority and charm.

In perfect French.

PART V

CLAIRE

MY CELL RINGS.

It's Ava.

"Just got some good news," she says cheerfully. She has made a big sale and is in a jubilant mood.

I congratulate her.

"Thanks. What's new with you, Claire?"

I decide not to bring her down by telling her about my surprise visit to Ray's gallery. Nor the dark revelation I experienced there. She wouldn't approve of the way I've let Ray's fluent French ignite my suspicion.

"Nothing new," I tell her.

"Really? Nothing at all? Even with Ray Patrick?"

"No."

"Or Simon?" Ava asks cautiously.

When I don't answer, Ava gets the message.

"What did you do this time?" she demands.

There is no point in evading her question.

"I tried to speak with Charlotte," I inform her. "To tell her about Simon. She wouldn't listen to me."

She is clearly aghast.

"Good God, Claire! You have to stop this. You have to wash your hands of him."

"If I do, he'll get what he wants."

"You don't know what he wants."

"Of course I know what he wants. Emma."

Ava offers no further argument. She's done her best to talk sense into me, and she's failed. In her view, I'm still the same old Claire. My own worst enemy. Tossing away any chance for happiness.

For the next few minutes we talk about other things. Ava avoids any further mention of Simon.

"I'd better go," I tell her finally. "I have a client."

"Yeah, okay," Ava says. I can hear the weariness in her voice. She's given up on trying to help me rid myself of what she considers a dangerous obsession.

It's a long drive to my next client. I make it through streets crowded with cars, past shops and strip malls filled with customers.

The city swarms around me.

But I have never felt more alone.

Chloé is my favorite client. She's thirteen years old. Her family is soon moving to France. Her house is on Elm Drive in Beverly Hills and is built in the style of a Tuscan country home, with a graceful colonnade at the front and large, arched windows. The yard is beautifully tended, with patches of flowers along the walkway.

Her mother greets me at the door. Her name is

Summer. She is always dressed in the colors of that season.

"My daughter is waiting for you in the courtyard," she tells me. "She really looks forward to these lessons, Claire."

Chloé is seated at a white wrought-iron table beneath a burgundy umbrella. She has long dark hair and blue eyes that shine with a lovely inner light.

"*Bonjour*," she says politely.

"*Bonjour*," I say, emphasizing a bit the explosive nature of the *bon* over the somewhat retiring *jour*.

Chloé hears the difference instantly. Then she repeats "*Bonjour*" correctly.

"*Très bien*," I tell her.

She beams. "*Merci beaucoup*."

There is an energy in this young girl, an eagerness to learn, that makes it a joy to teach her.

During the class I sometimes hear her mother moving about the house. Occasionally there is a male voice as well. The exchanges between Chloé's mother and father are casual and light-hearted. They often laugh.

A comforting playfulness reflects the mood of this home. It reminds me of the family I once had. Max and Melody. The simple things we enjoyed together. A day at the beach. A trip to the San Diego Zoo. *We were happy.* Melody was like Chloé, vibrant and hungry to learn. When

Max and I spoke to each other, it was always with humor and affection, as Chloé's parents do.

The time goes by rapidly, and an hour of French becomes ninety minutes of peace and pleasure.

Chloé walks me to the door. There is a small package on the table in the hallway. She hands it to me. "*C'est un cadeau pour vous*," she says. She has a gift for me.

It's a beautifully wrapped box of chocolates.

"*Oh, merci*," I tell Chloé. "*Comme c'est gentil.*"

I walk to my car and slide in behind the wheel. Chloé is still standing at the front door. She smiles brightly, waves, then steps inside.

I picture her returning to the courtyard, gathering up her notes or sitting down to study them, and it is a scene of such simple contentment, a teenage girl confident that she will never be betrayed, never disbelieved, never have reason to doubt her own mother.

Melody once had no such doubt.

As I drive away, I realize the extent to which a dream of happiness can motivate me.

I think of Melody.

She is four years old. We are having a picnic in Descanso Park. Melody takes a leaf, folds it delicately into her hair, then bends over one of the park's glassy ponds to catch a glimpse of herself in the water.

She lies in Angelus Rosedale Cemetery now. Unlike some LA cemeteries, this one is not dotted with the star-studded dead. No Marilyn Monroes or Elizabeth Taylors here, nor tourists seeking famous graves.

Melody's stone is as modest as the ones around it. Her name is engraved on it, along with the dates that encompassed her brief life. There is a small bench a few feet from where she rests. I come here once a month, and each time I bring a letter I've written to her. I read it silently, merely thinking the words. To anyone who might come by, I'm simply a woman sitting alone, reading to herself. But the words are for my daughter.

Dear Melody:

I remember that when you were afraid, you always wanted to hold my hand. Now I want to hold yours. I often imagine your eyes. I want to see them sparkling with life. With curiosity. I have beautiful memories of you talking with me, laughing with me, confiding in me. Even now I see you everywhere. In the morning, at first light. During the day, when I see other girls. At night, when I turn off the lamp. I want you to know that not a moment goes by when I'm not aware of the life you might have had and would still be having.

I am sorry.
Mom

SLOAN

THE COP IN **ME**.

What was it that still lingered with me from my days with the LAPD?

Maybe it was nothing more than the feeling that evil people should pay for the evil things they do.

You can leave the job, put your badge in a drawer and close it, but you can't put away the idea that bad people shouldn't just walk away from the pain they cause.

Remember Satan's feather.

It was only a small step from recalling my father's admonition to thinking about Vicki Page. If Destiny had told the truth, then a brothel that specialized in underage girls had been operating for years under her direction. I couldn't stand the thought of doing nothing with the information I'd gotten from Destiny.

I made a call to Candace. She had the necessary connections.

"What do you know about Vicki Page?" I asked.

She recognized the name. Everyone in the LAPD knew Vicki. She was a criminal legend in the department.

"Just that she's in the LAPD jail at the moment," she said. "She stabbed a woman on Venice Beach."

"Have you ever heard that she ran a brothel somewhere out in the desert? For men who are into young girls."

"No."

"Nothing at all?"

"I know she's been arrested for procurement, but that's ancient history. She's into more sophisticated stuff now. Identity theft, that sort of thing. Nothing about a brothel for pedophiles. Where'd you hear about this?"

"From someone I know who says she took the girl they found off Santa Monica Pier to Vicki and then went with both of them out to this place in the desert."

"Can you trust this someone?"

"I'm not sure. That's why I'd like to talk to Vicki. Can you get me in to see her?"

"You're not a cop anymore, Sloan," Candace reminded me.

"Part of me is."

Candace's tone went somber. "I see."

"Can you help me?"

"You know Vicki. She'll want something in return."

"What can I offer her?"

"You can tell her that if she talks to you, you'll have a word with me," Candace said. "And I'll put in a good word with someone else." She laughed. "They always take that bait."

She said she'd call the powers that be at the

jail, tell them that I wanted to see Vicki and make the offer.

Fifteen minutes later she got back to me.

"Vicki can't wait to see her old friend Detective Wilson," Candace said jokingly. "She's hoping for a real love fest." She laughed. "Actually she didn't want to talk to you at all, but she got the message, so she's willing. But don't expect much. She's a hard-ass."

That was true.

I'd dealt with Vicki before. None of those encounters had been pleasant. She'd been a hooker for a while but had long ago graduated to being a one-woman criminal enterprise. After that she'd run loan sharking operations, peddled prescription drugs, dabbled in identity theft, and subcontracted as a procurer for men with kinky sexual tastes. She was one of those people who never got up in the morning with the idea of making an honest living.

Later that morning I was waiting for her as she walked nonchalantly into one of the interrogation rooms at the jail, wearing a bright orange jumpsuit.

"Well, here she is," she said sarcastically. "Sloan Wilson, girl detective."

She feigned sudden surprise.

"Whoa. I forgot. You're not a cop anymore."

She dropped into a chair and stared at me

coldly. "Don't you look professional, all dolled up in your neat pantsuit."

I looked her up and down. "Orange is definitely your color, Vicki. My guess is you'll be wearing it for a long time."

Vicki smirked. "Beats copper blue."

That was Vicki to a T. Being hostile to anyone who wasn't as worthless as herself was all she knew of pride or self-respect.

"I hear you know something about the girl they found floating near the pier a few days ago." I opened the folder I'd brought and drew out a brief newspaper clipping about the discovery of the body of an unidentified girl off Santa Monica Pier.

Vicki gave it an indifferent glance, then turned it facedown on the table. "I don't read the paper unless I'm mentioned in it."

"You have no idea who this girl might be?"

"Let me guess. Jane Doe Two Million?"

She sat back in her chair and folded her arms over her chest. She looked like the queen of criminals sitting on her throne.

"I shouldn't be in this shithole," she said in a way that made it clear that as far as she was concerned, the subject of the drowned girl was now closed. "I didn't stab that bitch for nothing. She got what was coming to her. She started it. She's the one who should be in this fucking jail."

She said this in an aggrieved tone, like an

honest businesswoman burdened by unjust competition. That was what my father had hated about people like Vicki. They all believed they were somehow the wounded party.

Vicki laughed. "You must be doing good, though. Most cops that leave the job end up night watchmen in warehouses or providing security for big-shot weddings. That's what cops do, right? When they're not on the job anymore. Ain't that what your dear old daddy did when he left off being a real cop?"

"What my father did is no concern of yours," I told her sternly.

Vicki sat back with a sneer. "Well, all dressed up like you are, I figure you must have found something better."

"I do private work," I told her. "That's all you need to know."

Vicki released a bored sigh. "What do you want . . . Detective?" she asked.

"The girl in the newspaper. You farmed her out to a bunch of creeps."

"Where did you hear that?"

"From one of your girls."

Vicki grinned confidently. "My 'girls,' as you put it, don't rat on me."

"One of them did. She says you specialize in underage girls."

Vicki's expression turned lethal.

"You take them to a house in the desert," I

added. "Someplace in the middle of nowhere."

Vicki stared at me with a brittle invulnerability. "What do you care? You're not a cop anymore. It's none of your business what I do."

She leaned forward and something poisonous came into her eyes.

"Listen up," she said sharply. "If you keep sniffing around with that cop nose of yours, you're going to get hurt real bad."

She looked at me as if she were suddenly in charge.

"I know plenty . . . Detective. Plenty you don't want to hear, or have anyone else hear."

I knew what she was getting at. She was telling me that she had something on me from my days with the LAPD, that I was corrupt and that she knew it. Since everyone was on the take in one way or another, I had to have been dirty, too. She didn't need to be specific. I would get the message.

But I'd never taken a bribe or done an inappropriate favor. I had nothing to fear from her.

I called her bluff.

"You're full of shit," I said.

She stood her ground, and added a twisted little smile.

"I'm telling you to forget about that girl. That house in the desert. Along with anything else that snitch told you. Back away, or you'll be sorry."

She made me sick.

I got up and headed out of the room.

"You're going down, Sloan," Vicki called when I reached the door.

I looked at her.

"No, Vicki. You are."

I walked out of the building and had nearly reached my car when I heard a voice behind me.

"How's the incorruptible Detective Wilson?"

I turned to see a local drug dealer named Darrell Smithers, a psychopathic thug whose competition was often found in the trunks of stolen cars.

"You are looking fine, mama," Smithers said. "Pity you're wasting all that good stuff."

It was impossible to know just how much damage he had done during the course of his worthless life. How many people he'd maimed or murdered. How many children had been shot in the drive-bys he'd ordered. He was a poisonous little snake who'd slither through Los Angeles for as long as he drew breath.

His gaze moved up and down my body. "Mighty good stuff."

He was all smiles and relaxation. He could wink at me, leer at me, and make suggestive remarks. There was nothing I could do. He knew this, and relied upon it to protect himself from the anger he provoked.

"Mighty fine," he repeated in a lascivious tone.

When I reached for the door handle of my car,

he laughed. "You should come home with me, girl," he said in a mocking voice. "You should come home to Daddy."

The impulse that swept over me was so strong it all but lifted me into the air. I wanted to take him by the throat and squeeze until he turned blue, watch his mouth foam until he died like a dog on the pavement.

Instead I got into my car and drove to my office.

Once there, I called Destiny.

"I want to find the house where you took the girl," I told her.

Destiny caught her breath.

"I don't know where it is," she said.

"You know the general area. We'll look until we find it."

She knew I wasn't going to let this go. "I could try, I guess," she said weakly. "But what's it got to do with—"

I cut her off.

"What time are you off today?"

"Four this afternoon."

"I'll be there."

Two hours later she came out of 24/7, craning her neck, looking for my car. When she saw it, she walked toward me quickly and got in.

"I may not be able to find it," she said.

"You'll find it," I told her. "Because if you

don't, I'll tell Vicki Page you snitched on her."

Destiny froze.

"We both know what'll happen to you after that," I said.

She nodded meekly.

"I'll show you where it is."

She directed me to the 10-E out of Los Angeles. An hour later we nosed into the desert. There were a few small dusty crossroads with a gas station and what amounted to a general store, but it was mostly scrub brush, rock, and sand. I spotted a coyote in the distance. It was scrawny and probably covered in vermin. It looked like the land around it, thirsty and deprived.

"Take a right here," she said after we'd driven into the desert for another half hour.

I turned onto a weedy road. Pale green cacti rose into the bleached air. I caught sight of a few rolling balls of desiccated brush. No one lived out this way anymore, but there were a couple of tumbledown shacks, long abandoned. As we drove, the road steadily narrowed until it became little more than two bone-dry ruts across the desert floor.

At last it came to an end at the dilapidated gate of a farmhouse.

"That's it," Destiny said.

I gazed silently at the house. It was a wreck. Clearly no one had lived in it for years. But what got my attention in that jumble of wood and cracked glass was that the windows were black and the door was red.

"Is this . . . McDuffy's?"

"Yes," Destiny answered.

She looked at me pointedly.

"Vicki saw it," she said. "She thought it was the girl's way of trying to tell people about what had happened to her."

The grim implication was obvious.

"Did Vicki have her killed?" I asked.

Destiny looked both sad for the girl and frightened for herself.

"I don't know. Really. I don't know."

We got out of the car and walked to the house. Just to be safe, I knocked, then, when there was no sign of anyone inside, I tried the door. It wasn't locked.

The front room had been stripped of anything that might leave a trace of who'd been here or for what reason. Everything had been cleaned thoroughly, every piece of furniture removed. There'd be no fingerprints here. No DNA. It was as if the whole house had just descended from the big sky above, had never felt a human touch.

Staring at this room, I knew that there'd be no sign of where the girl in the water had lain, drugged and insensible, waiting to be raped. All evidence of her ordeal had been wiped away as completely as her body had been washed in the sea.

I couldn't help but wonder if I might have saved her, along with others Vicki had brought here, if I'd stayed a cop.

I remembered the morning I'd decided to leave the LAPD. I'd been at my desk for only a few minutes when a call came in.

"It's a family thing, Sloan," the dispatcher said gravely.

Family things always got to me, particularly the cruelest domestics, the ones that turned dark and bloody.

"Wife and two kids," the dispatcher added. "Over on Sepulveda."

I recognized the house the minute we pulled up to it. I'd been called there several times. Always by neighbors who'd heard a woman screaming, children crying.

There were squad cars everywhere, along with a couple of ambulances waiting to take the bodies away. There were three of them. A woman facedown on the kitchen floor. A girl around nine years old on the living room sofa. Another, two years younger, in the hallway. The woman and one of the girls had been shot in the back of the head. The other daughter, the older one, had been shot in the throat and the chest.

"I've been here a few times," I told one of the other detectives. "The name's Bennett, right?"

"That's right. They're holding him in the back-yard."

Bennett stood surrounded by a few cops, some in uniform, some in plain clothes. His hands were cuffed behind him. He was dressed in black trousers and a white sleeveless T-shirt. His face was red and his eyes were watery.

When he saw me, there was a glimmer of recognition.

"Annie saw it coming," he said to no cop in particular. "The others, it was in the back. They didn't know what hit them. But Annie saw me with the gun and just stood there. Like she didn't get it. Maybe it was a joke. Like it couldn't be real." He peered about wonderingly. "She just stood there. 'Dad?' she said. 'Dad?'"

He rambled on, sometimes stopping for a teary interval. As he talked, I recalled the times I'd been here. The cringing of the wife. The terror in the faces of the little girls who clung to her legs. I knew the world they'd cowered in.

Now Bennett's tale careened into self-pity.

It was always the same story. I'd heard it a thousand times.

He was under a lot of pressure, poor thing.

His wife was always complaining and the girls were always fighting.

How much of this was a man supposed to take?

Anybody can snap, right?

It turned my stomach.

I wanted to bring him to his knees, make

him beg for his life: *This is how it feels to be terrorized.*

But everything said, *Go by the rules.*

I walked back into the house, stood in the hallway, and tried to get a grip. I could feel a rattling inside me, like a house rocked by wind, small pieces coming loose, flying away. I had to gather them back in.

For God's sake, calm down, I told myself.

That had been the moment when I'd known I had to leave the job.

Now I felt my old career summon me back.

I wanted to bring Vicki Page down, and seized by that passion, I thought of all the times my father must have felt the same way. That was what my mother's denunciation and later suicide had finally done to him. They had denied him his calling, separated him from all the good he might have done.

My old resentment of my mother seized me.

I all but vibrated with a ferocious need to make her pay.

She was well beyond my reach, however. Claire Fontaine came into my sights instead. It was as if they'd merged, become inseparable.

I knew that my first strategy for silencing Claire had failed. Destiny had found nothing I could use against Claire.

As I drove back to LA, with Destiny sitting silently beside me, I searched for a scheme that would shut Claire down once and for all.

Since Destiny hadn't gotten anything on Claire, the new strategy couldn't rely on dredging up some shameful aspect of her past.

The next device had to come entirely out of left field.

I had to think outside the usual sin-eater box, come up with something bold and clever and totally unexpected, a twist in the story that would completely surprise Claire, change any notion she'd earlier had of what was actually going on and at the same time draw her yet more firmly under my control.

By the time I got back to Los Angeles, I'd found it.

CLAIRE

I AM JUST getting to my first client's house when my phone rings.

It's Ray.

I don't answer it.

A few seconds later there is a text message.

Claire? Tried to call you. Everything okay?

Nothing is okay.

Why would Ray hire me under such false pretenses? He doesn't need a French teacher. What's his game?

Game.

Even the word suggests a hidden hand.

I tell myself that it has nothing to do with Simon.

As far as I know, Simon hasn't done anything in the wake of my meeting with Charlotte.

But he will.

I know he will.

It's only a matter of time.

I arrive at Margot's house just after ten in the morning.

When she opens the door, I know something's wrong. She steps out of the light, her head bowed. When she looks up, I see that she's applied a great deal of makeup, particularly around the purplish bruises at her right eye and in two long, smudgy lines circling her throat.

"I didn't want to cancel."

She closes the door and escorts me to the dining room, where she has already placed various materials.

I sit down opposite her and pretend not to see the obvious signs of the beating she has taken. Her bottom lip is cracked and swollen, and a scratch, red and jagged, stretches from the corner of her right eye into the hairline at the side of her head.

"Are you ready to begin?" I ask her.

"Yes."

I start with a few very simple questions that require her to practice the three tenses she is learning.

As she answers, she keeps her eyes lowered and responds in a soft voice. She says nothing about her bruises. I don't mention them either.

I am her French teacher, after all, not her guardian. She has given me no indication that she wants help. I suspect that she is fixed in the notion that somehow something will change, though I suspect it won't.

I fashion the lesson in a way that I hope will be sensitive to her situation. In French, I ask her what she will do on Monday.

She answers that she will cook dinner.

I ask her what she will do in winter.

She says she will buy warm clothes.

I ask her to tell me about her future, hoping that it will jar her into seriously considering it.

She answers in generalities about having children, going on vacations, growing old, responses that give no hint of how the violence in her life profoundly contradicts the idyllic future that is only in her head.

At the end of the lesson, I hand her new vocabulary sheets.

She walks me to the door. "Thank you," she says.

I feel a final urge to intervene. I want to tell her that she can call me, that I will help her if she needs me.

Instead I watch as Margot shrinks back into the house and closes the door.

On the way to my next client, I keep thinking about Margot. I should have let her know that I was aware of her situation, perhaps looked up a hotline number and given it to her.

My phone rings.

It's Julie Cooper.

"I have to tell you something, Claire," she says. "I'm not what or who you think I am."

Her tone is strained yet tender, the voice of confession.

"My name isn't Julie Cooper."

She sounds very grave.

"I'm not a writer."

There is a note of shame in her tone.

"I work for Simon."

I am stunned. I can hardly breathe.

"My name is Sloan Wilson."

SLOAN

IT ISN'T LONELINESS that destroys human beings.

It's broken trust.

They can handle solitude, shattered dreams, all manner of failure, as long as they don't feel completely betrayed.

I was betting that since Claire felt herself deceived, or at least disbelieved, by just about everyone, she might see me as her only remaining ally.

She was silent after I told her my name.

I waited a few seconds before I added, "The day you brought Destiny in, you asked me whether I ever just had a feeling about something. As it turned out, I got a feeling about Simon. So I studied your records. What you said about him five years ago."

I took the sort of pause that leaves the listener in rapt anticipation of what comes next.

"And the thing is . . . I believe you, Claire."

I paused before making the ultimate reversal.

"I'm working for you now."

I made it sound like we were sisters-in-arms, two woman warriors pitted against Evil Simon.

As a final thrust, I added the fearlessness and determination she'd want in an ally.

"Together," I told her in a voice so steadfast and unyielding she couldn't possibly doubt my resolve.

I waited for her to respond, but she didn't. "Together," I repeated.

Then once more, this time quite forcefully.

"Together, Claire."

I called Simon an hour later.

"It's Sloan," I said when he answered. "I'd like to talk to you."

Simon heard the gravity in my voice.

"Face-to-face, I take it?" he asked.

"Yes."

"Okay, how about the Grove? Bar Verde. On the patio. I can meet you there in an hour."

When he arrived, he was dressed somberly, in a dark suit.

"What happened?" he said as he sat down.

I told him that I'd turned the tables on Claire. She now thought I'd come over to her side, a strategy that would allow me to keep a closer eye on her as well as have more power over what she thought or did.

Simon was clearly troubled by this change in direction.

"Be careful," he said. "Because she can be very persuasive."

He seemed seized by the need to explain himself once again.

"Imagine. You're sitting in the cabin of a boat. Suddenly your wife comes in and tells you that your stepdaughter has accused you of being a creep. I was horrified. All I could do was deny it. How could I prove I'd never touched or looked at Melody in a bad way? I'm sure you know what I mean, given your father's experience. The accusation is enough."

He shook his head.

"I can barely stand to remember this."

His hurt gave way to a deep sadness.

"I loved Melody," he said. "She was like my own daughter."

"What did you say to Claire when she confronted you that night?"

A sense of futility settled over him. He was like a man defending a fortress alone, with the enemy on all sides.

"I told her it wasn't true, and that she was crazy to believe it. Melody was a teenager. She had . . . 'raging hormones.' Isn't that the phrase? Who knows what she was capable of coming up with?"

He paused briefly before he added, "Claire listened, then turned and left the cabin. I saw her pass the window a few times. She was searching everywhere. But Melody had already gotten into the dinghy." He looked as fully tortured by Melody's subsequent death as Claire. "It was too late."

He'd spewed all this out spontaneously.

At the end he looked exhausted.

"Anyway," he said, "be careful with Claire. She can be very . . . manipulative. When she tells you things, you might be tempted to believe her."

"Nothing could make me believe her," I assured him.

Simon smiled.

"Good," he said. "I'm glad to hear it."

He looked at me pointedly.

"I'm sure you didn't call me here just to tell me that you were making friends with Claire. You could have said that over the phone."

"You're right, there's something else," I said. "I'm going to draw her into a plot."

Simon was intrigued.

"Really? What kind?"

"Murder," I said.

He laughed, thinking this was a joke.

When my expression remained dead serious, he asked, "Who's she planning to kill?"

"You."

He looked at me uneasily.

"If I can get her on tape in a murder-for-hire scheme, then we'll have something to use against her," I explained. "It doesn't have to be all that much. No money has to change hands. It's just something you can use to get, say, a very tough restraining order against her. The sort that if she breaks it, she could be arrested on the spot, go right to jail. Given what happened to her last time, that possibility should get her attention."

Simon smiled. "It's not a plot to kill me," he said flippantly.

"No, it's only a tactic for silencing her. No one else will be involved. Just Claire and me. Two voices on a wire. If I can get her on tape discussing a murder, then I'll have a gun to her head. She either shuts her mouth or ends up in serious trouble. That's all you want, isn't it? To shut her up?"

He nodded. "Yeah, that's all I want. For Claire to be . . . silent."

I expected Simon to probe a bit for what I had in mind, but instead he called the waiter over and ordered two glasses of champagne.

"We have something to celebrate."

He drew a photograph from his suit pocket.

"This is the award," he told me. "The Monroe Wilson Scholarship."

In the picture Simon is holding a large drawing. It is a mock-up of a brass statue of my father in uniform. Standing tall. Looking proud. Exactly the way I remembered him.

"We can give the statue with the scholarship," Simon said. "The recipient will always have it. Like an Oscar."

I was pleased by how powerfully the figure of my father brought back memories.

"You can keep the picture," Simon said.

When the champagne arrived, he lifted his glass.

"To your dad."

After we drank, Simon offered another toast, this one almost whimsical. "And to our success in getting rid of Claire."

We went our separate ways a few minutes later.

Once in my car, I placed the picture on the passenger seat. From time to time, as I drove home, I glanced at it, and felt almost as if my father had returned to me, was riding beside me, as if we were partners on the job.

CLAIRE

THE NEXT MORNING I replay my conversation with Sloan. Her strength is like solid ground beneath me.

Firm.

Supportive.

A cautious hope envelops me.

I expect it quickly to dissipate, but it lingers throughout the day. It is almost as if she is at my side, my partner, as it were, in crime.

I'm in the middle of my last lesson of the day when the phone rings.

Normally I don't answer calls while I'm teaching, but caller ID tells me that it is Dr. Aliabadi.

"Excuse me," I tell my student, then immediately answer the phone.

"Your father isn't doing very well," the doctor says. "You should come to the hospital."

She doesn't go into detail with regard to his condition, but I can hear the urgency in her voice.

"All right. I'll get there as soon as I can."

I stop my class and rush to the hospital. On the way to my father's room, I see Dr. Aliabadi near the nurses' station.

"How is he?"

She shakes her head.

"There's nothing more we can do. His heart is worn out."

He is awake when I come into the room.

When he sees me, he closes his eyes. I settle into the chair near his bed.

A couple of hours go by before I get up and walk out into the corridor. I turn to the right and move down the hallway. Some of the rooms have their doors open. I get glimpses of patients and their families.

Suddenly I see her. Margot.

She is lying on her back. There are bandages along the side of her head and another across her nose. Her eyes are black and her lips are so swollen they no longer look human. Tubes run from the respirator to her mouth and nose.

I am mortified.

When a nurse approaches, I introduce myself and tell her that I'm a French teacher and that Margot is one of my clients.

"Is she going to be all right?"

"I don't know," the nurse answers.

I look back into the room and wonder if I could have stopped this if I'd talked to her. But I didn't, and now it's too late.

Too late.

Is that the theme of my life, its unending refrain—that I can't trust myself to do the right thing? It's dangerous to feel this way. An undermining that could cause me to collapse, to surrender.

Je me bats, I remind myself. I am fighting.

But I need an ally.

I call Ava but get only her voicemail.

I don't leave a message because I know that the tone of my voice would alarm her.

That's when I think of Sloan.

Our latest conversation.

The last word she'd said to me. *Together.*

I dial her number. When she answers, I say, "I hope you don't mind me calling you."

"Of course not," Sloan assures me. "What's the matter? You sound . . . stressed."

"I let someone down."

"Who?"

"One of my students. I let her down."

"What happened, Claire?"

"I was too late for her."

"In what way?"

"I knew her husband had hit her and I should have . . ."

"Where are you, Claire?"

"At the hospital in Marina Del Ray."

"Meet me at the cafeteria. I'm on my way."

I'm on my way. Sloan's voice is strong, her reaction immediate.

Some friends are like first responders. When you call them in an emergency, they come as fast as they can.

286

SLOAN

CLAIRE HAD NEVER sounded more distressed. She was in the middle of a crisis. She hadn't acted in time. Someone had suffered as a result. That was all I knew, but it was enough.

It didn't matter what Claire had done or failed to do. The point was that it had really upset her. Which provided the perfect opportunity for me to initiate my plan to incriminate her.

To make the most of this situation, I quickly went to my car and headed for the hospital.

Claire was sitting in the cafeteria when I arrived. She was fidgeting with a cup of coffee. Her nerves were on edge, and there was a jittery agitation in her eyes.

"I should have done something, Sloan," she said.

"Tell me exactly what happened."

"Margot, one of my clients, is here," Claire told me. "Her husband beat her up. I knew it was going to happen, but I didn't do anything about it. And now she's . . ."

She was clearly ashamed of whatever she'd done—or failed to do. She was both angry and disappointed in herself.

A friend would have taken Claire's hand and insisted that none of this was her fault. But I wasn't her friend. I wanted her to continue to blame herself for this beating, accuse herself of being weak, hesitant, always too late.

I kept quiet as Claire went through the details. She talked about how she'd seen the bruises on Margot's face and immediately known their cause. Which was Margot's husband. She'd thought about confronting the situation head-on, perhaps giving Margot the number of some service that might help. Instead she'd done nothing. The result being that Margot was now barely hanging on to life.

I just listened, because I knew it was better to let Claire stew in these juices for a while. To offer any relief would lessen the internal pressure she was feeling.

Once she'd finished telling me all this, she said, "I want to see Margot."

We headed for the elevator and got off on the fourth floor. I followed her down the corridor and into a room where a woman lay unconscious. She looked like she'd either been in a car accident or been badly beaten.

"I let this happen," Claire told me.

She was at rock bottom now.

"Let's go back downstairs," I said. We turned and headed to the elevator.

Once we were in the cafeteria again, I was careful to guide her to a table in the far corner.

On the way, I didn't say a word.

After we'd taken our seats, Claire folded her hands in front of her.

"What now?" she asked.

"What do you mean?"

"Will her husband be arrested?"

"He's probably already been arrested."

"And he'll spend, what? A few nights in jail?"

"That depends."

"On what?"

"Mostly on how much your client wants to make the case against him."

Claire shook her head.

"If she goes back to him, he'll do it again."

She looked at me angrily.

"That's what they bet on, isn't it? That we'll convince ourselves it was just this one time. It'll never happen again. They depend on us accepting that lie. They know we won't stop them."

And I thought, *Now.*

"Anyone can be stopped," I told her matter-of-factly. "But doing it can have serious consequences."

As if I were only describing a routine business experience, I said, "I knew a woman who killed her husband. He'd been beating her for years. She finally took a knife and cut his throat while he was dead drunk on the living room sofa. She seemed to think that would be the end of the story. But it wasn't. It was murder. She got fifteen years in prison. The same could happen to Margot."

"Margot's already in prison," Claire said grimly. "Every day. Just knowing her husband's alive and he can do whatever he wants."

I let a second or two go by before I set the snare I had in mind.

"A man can be prevented from getting what he wants," I said. "But it shouldn't be the woman who does it. Not the wife, I mean."

Claire looked at me quizzically.

In a tone that indicated I knew more than the price of having someone murdered, I added, "It has to be someone else. Someone she doesn't know. A professional."

Claire's eyes flashed. "A . . . professional?"

"That's right."

I thought Claire might take the bait, or at least ask another question. Instead she drew in a taut breath and got to her feet.

"Thanks for coming, Sloan," she said.

I didn't want to leave her. There was a chance she wouldn't call me again.

"Do you want to go somewhere else?" I asked. "Have a drink?"

She shook her head. "My father's here. He had a heart attack. That's why I was here. Otherwise I wouldn't have known about Margot."

"I see," I said quietly. I waited a beat. "Look, if you're father's still in the hospital, I could meet

290

you here tomorrow night. We could just talk."

She seemed hesitant to accept my offer.

"It's what friends do, Claire," I added.

She smiled softly. "Okay. Tomorrow."

On the way to my car, it struck me that during our discussion about Margot, her husband, women who let men get away with it, Claire had not once mentioned Simon. That didn't matter. Claire's failure with Margot had almost certainly got her thinking about her failure to save Melody, along with the possibility that she would also be too late to rescue Emma from the evil clutches of Simon Miller. If she kept accusing herself of these self-lacerating disappointments, she'd surely arrive at the conclusion that the time had come to act.

The next time we meet, I told myself, *I'll wear a wire.*

CLAIRE

THE NEXT MORNING I call the hospital. My father has stabilized. He is sleeping. They will let me know if his condition changes. I decide not to cancel any clients for the moment.

For the next few hours I teach one student, then another. I practice vocabulary and conjugate verbs and go through lessons prepared beforehand for scores of clients over the years.

It's my usual routine, but nothing is the same.

Margot's beaten body.

My inaction about Simon.

I'm genuinely frightened of what I'm thinking, of how far I might actually go to stop him.

These thoughts create an urge to see Emma, so in the afternoon I park my car across the street from her school and wait for it to let out. When it does, a stream of girls pour through the wide doors. They scatter in various directions after they pass through the gate. They are rushing to the waiting cars of their parents.

Emma is in a small knot of girls. They are all in same neat uniform, a gray skirt and white polo. She is blond, and the bright light of Los Angeles turns her hair to gold. She is laughing and tossing her head. The world is hers, as it had once been Melody's.

I am enjoying this vision of Emma until I see Simon.

He is standing beside his car, motioning to her as she leaves the school grounds.

His smile is warm and welcoming, as always.

When Emma spots him, she quickly says good-bye to her friends and rushes toward him, happy and trusting.

Others would see a happy little girl rushing toward a beloved father.

I see Simon's next victim.

Mr. Cohen is sitting alone in his yard when I pull into my drive after a day of work.

He waves at me.

I don't want to talk to anyone, but he is a lonely man, so I walk over to him.

"How's your father?" he asks with a hint of worry.

"Still in the hospital."

"Will he be going home soon?"

"I don't know."

I notice the book on Mr. Cohen's lap. A biography of Joan of Arc.

"A brave woman," Mr. Cohen says.

My indifference to Joan of Arc's courage surprises and troubles me. I realize that I am no longer capable of being engaged by anything beyond my own future action. The world has shrunk to the narrow space that separates me from Simon. I can think of nothing else. He is the furiously overheated room I can't get out of. Even in open air I feel trapped.

"Give your father my best," Mr. Cohen tells me.

"I will."

I walk into my office. I don't feel like preparing lessons. I sit behind my desk and let my gaze wander.

Eventually my attention falls on one of the prints I've hung across from my desk. It is the famous trompe l'oeil by Pere Borrell De Caso. It shows a young boy attempting to flee the painting's frame. It's called *Escaping Criticism*, and I've always found it a whimsical and uplifting work.

Now it seems like a taunt.

A cruel lie.

For there is no escape.

No escape at all.

SLOAN

AS WE'D AGREED the night before, Claire was waiting for me at the same table in the hospital cafeteria.

A few minutes earlier I'd readied a voice-activated recording device. The days of people wearing dangerously bulky recorders were long past. Mine was the size of a shirt button, easily hidden by the lapel of my jacket.

When I spotted Claire in the far corner of the room, I could see that she was in the same pent-up, explosive condition she'd been in the night before.

"I went to Emma's school today," she said tensely when I sat down across from her. "Simon was there to pick her up."

She took a deep breath before she added, "I can't let him do it again, Sloan."

Without being asked, she launched into her tale of the night Melody died. It was raining and the sea was rough.

Claire was on the deck, heading toward the cabin she shared with Simon, when she saw Melody standing by the rail.

"She looked sick," Claire said. "I thought maybe it was the rocking of the boat. I asked her if she was okay. She didn't answer right away.

Finally she said, 'No, Mom. I'm not okay.' "

Claire stared at me stonily.

"She told me that Simon was attracted to her. And it wasn't just a matter of glances. When he hugged her, it was too hard, too long. The way he looked at her made her cringe. And once he came up behind her, pressed against her, and she'd . . . felt him."

She shook her head.

"She told me all of this, and you know what I said to her? That I didn't believe her. Then I went to our cabin and told Simon what Melody had said. He looked at me like I was crazy to believe anything Melody told me. He was the innocent victim of a false accusation. Melody was going through a phase. It was as simple as that."

She regarded me without a hint of doubt as to the truth of what she said next.

"But he was the liar, not Melody. And he would have gone further. Or at least tried. He would have seduced her if he could. He may have done it before, to some other little girl. And I know he'll do it again. Because that's what he is. A child molester."

It was clear by her expression and the melancholy tenor of her voice that Claire's delusions had completely taken over. She was carved from their falsehood, a product of their sinister intrigue.

"He'll do it again," she repeated. "Unless I stop him."

She took a sip of the coffee she'd been nursing before I joined her at the table. Her eyes were red-rimmed and watery. She was completely depleted, with her back to the wall.

"I guess that in the end it comes down to how far a person is willing to go," I told her.

She nodded.

She was getting close to the edge. A few more words in this direction and I'd have her on tape discussing the murder-for-hire killing of Simon Miller. *Come on now,* I thought. *Let's go just a little further down this road.*

I watched patiently as she turned things over in her mind. I needed her to take the next step. But she didn't.

Instead, she lifted her head, almost proudly, like a soldier returning to the battle. "I should get back up to my father's room," she said.

The night before, she'd evaded any further discussion of this subject by the same means of escape, but now I was too close to carrying out my plan to release her.

"I'll go with you," I said quickly.

We got to our feet and a couple of minutes later entered her father's room. Claire walked over to his bed.

She was infinitely sad.

For a moment she watched her father silently.

Then she turned toward me very quickly, almost violently. "What do you think of me, Sloan?" she asked.

I was about to assure her that I respected her. That I sympathized with her. If it worked, she'd finally trust me enough to discuss murdering Simon Miller.

But a doctor opened the door of the room. "Do you have a minute, Ms. Fontaine?"

Claire followed the doctor out into the corridor, leaving me alone with the old man.

He was lying on his back. His eyes were closed, but there was a lot of movement beneath the lids. Quick darting motions, like someone looking for an exit. A few seconds later he opened his eyes and took a quick breath. "Ah!" he gasped loudly, like a man coming up for air. His eyes were aflame.

I stepped over to the bed.

He reached out in my direction, his fingers grasping. I gave him my hand. He clutched my wrist brutally. I looked toward the door of the room, hoping to see Claire come through it. When she didn't, I returned my attention to him. "I'm here," I told him.

At the sound of my voice, something went cold in him, as if he were a man steadying himself for a fatal move.

"You," he snarled. "You . . ."

He jerked my arm vehemently, his fingers closed around my wrist like steel bands.

"You . . ."

He was tugging viciously, a hard downward pull, as if I were hanging above him and he was determined to pull me free of whatever I clung to.

"You . . . cunt."

I instantly recalled Simon's story of what had happened to Claire as a child. He had framed it as a lie, one of her delusions. Now I knew the terrible truth. Claire's father had never stopped wanting her dead.

I pulled free of him and stepped back from the bed.

He reached for me desperately, each thrust weaker than the one before until his arms finally dropped to his sides.

After that, I retreated to the window. I was still there when Claire came back into the room.

She immediately saw the anxiety in my eyes. "Are you all right?"

"Yeah," I answered, "I'm fine."

But I wasn't. Because I could still feel the iron clasp of her father's hand, his fingers like metal teeth. Even at death's door he was grabbing for her ankles, dragging her from the boat and into the water.

I felt a wave of horror. I had to get out of this room.

"I'll leave you now, Claire," I said.

She smiled. "Thanks for coming."

As I walked to the door, she faced her father and in a tentative gesture reached out a comforting hand. I thought she was going to touch him tenderly, but as her hand got closer, it began to tremble, and it kept trembling until she drew it back and sank it into the pocket of her dress.

2.

Back at my house, I poured a drink and sat down on the sofa in the living room.

I could still feel the old man's murderous grip.

How many years had Claire lived in dread of him, her childhood so marked by fear that even now, as a grown woman, he terrified her?

I was on my second glass when the phone rang. It was Destiny.

"Can I talk to you?" she asked. "Please, can we meet?"

She was quite agitated, and when people are strung out, they are prone to do dangerous and unpredictable things. I decided to calm her down.

"Okay, I'll meet you at the usual place."

An hour later I pulled into the parking lot of 24/7. Destiny came out of the restaurant and walked directly to my car. She looked shaken, distracted.

"I have to talk to you," she said as she snatched the photograph Simon had given me from the passenger seat and slid it onto the dash, then slumped into the seat.

"What's this all about?" I asked once she'd closed the door.

"I'm afraid of Vicki," she said. "Because I know she'll kill me if she finds out I've talked to you. She hates snitches. She gives long talks about how much she hates them."

She was scared out of her mind.

"Please, you have to promise me that you won't tell Vicki."

"Vicki's in jail at the moment," I said. "She stabbed another woman."

"She killed her?" Destiny asked in a tone that sounded almost hopeful, as if this was the answer to her prayers.

"No, it was only a flesh wound," I told her.

"Then she'll get out at some point."

"Yes, she will."

"I can't let that happen."

"What do you mean?"

"I have to make sure she stays in jail."

"How can you do that?"

"I could make sure she's charged with something else."

"What?"

"Like maybe . . . farming out underage girls. Like, sex trafficking. I could tell the cops she did that. And if I did that, maybe, as a witness, I could . . . you know . . . walk away?"

"That's possible," I said. "But you'd better have your facts straight, Destiny."

"What does that mean?"

"It means you'd better have real evidence on

Vicki. Something strong enough that you could make a deal."

I could see that Destiny was turning this over in her mind. Finally she said, "I have enough."

"You were involved?"

"A little, but Vicki ran things. I was just a . . ."

"A what?"

"Like . . . an assistant."

The story she related during the next few minutes was bad even by LA standards. The house in the desert was a regular meeting place for Vicki and her numerous clients. It had been a makeshift brothel for years. Recently the clientele had become more specialized, with a taste for younger girls. Often the girls were foreign, with no English. They were taken to the house, used, then returned to their keepers. Others were local, recruited from the streets, then returned to them.

"The girls were always changing," she said. "Sometimes they'd just show up once."

Destiny suspected that some of the girls lived on the road, kept in vans that moved from city to city. It might have gone on forever, but the girl in the water had complicated things, and so Vicki had shut the operation down.

"Maybe it'll start up again once things cool off," Destiny added. "But I won't have anything to do with it, I swear."

Destiny's newfound virtue didn't interest me.

"Keep going," I said.

She did. As she continued to talk, more details about how things operated at what she suddenly called "Lolitaville" came to light.

"We'd go with a few of them," Destiny said. "Once we got there, Vicki would take the first girl inside the house."

"Where were you?"

"I stayed in the van with the other girls, keeping an eye on them. Like a guard, you might say. But I didn't hit them. I never hit any of them."

Destiny clearly considered this proof of her good character.

"You didn't need to do that, really," she added. "Because once they were in the van, they couldn't put up much of a fight."

"Why not?"

"Because before we left LA, Vicki drugged them," Destiny answered. "Not heavy stuff, though. Vicki didn't want them to be zombies. She wanted them easy to handle. No yelling. No crying. No punching us or trying to run off. They had to be lively enough to please her customers. I mean, what's the point, if they're just dead weight?"

Once again I kept it low-key, as if I were simply evaluating the quality of her testimony.

"Nothing more than drugs?" I asked. "That's all she used to control them?"

"No, she handcuffed them," Destiny answered.

"The ones she left inside, I mean. Then she'd come out and get the next one."

"You never went inside?"

Destiny shook her head. "I was just a guard."

From the way she said this, you'd have thought she worked in security at a department store.

"After we got them all inside, men would show up," she continued. "They'd choose the girl they liked, do what they wanted with her, then stroll back to their cars and take off back to LA or wherever they'd come from." She took out a cigarette and lit it. "Vicki had a real strict schedule worked out. A guy was on the clock from the minute he showed up. Vicki, she didn't give an extra second. When someone's time was up, his time was up, and off he'd go."

She slapped her hands together.

"Over and out, know what I mean?"

"What happened to the girls after that?"

"When it was over, I'd take them back to the van," Destiny answered. "I'd talk nice to them. Tell them everything was fine. Give them something to eat and drink."

She seemed to think her simple helpfulness made her a better person.

"How long did you do this?" I asked.

"Until that girl showed up in the water. I figured Vicki was responsible, and I said to myself, *Don't ever have anything else to do with her.*"

305

"Did Vicki have something to do with that girl's death?"

Destiny looked at me meaningfully. "Vicki could do anything. And painting that picture on the wall near McDuffy's, where anybody could see it—Vicki wouldn't like that."

She shrugged.

"I'm not saying Vicki killed her. Or had her killed. But with Vicki, you never know."

When I had no more questions, she slapped her hands together almost playfully. "I guess that's it," she said. "That's what I've got. It's a lot, right?"

"Yes, but maybe not enough."

She was surprised to hear this.

"They'll need names, Destiny," I told her.

She thought this requirement over before making her decision. "I guess I could do that," she said finally. She smiled nervously. "Can you help me?" she asked. "You must know people."

"I'll do the best I can," I assured her.

She looked as if I'd just pulled her head out of a tiger's mouth. "Thanks. Because Vicki would kill me or have me killed by one of her goons."

She pulled out a pack of cigarettes.

"You mind?" she asked lightly, as if we were now just two old friends having a chat.

"Go ahead."

She lit a cigarette and leaned back. In no hurry to leave. She looked down the street.

"One day I'd like a nice little house," she said.

She was entirely at ease now, making herself at home in my car.

"What happened to you?" I asked.

"What do you mean?"

"That you ended up living on the street. Working for Vicki Page."

"The usual routine. Mom on dope. With her boyfriend more interested in me than her. I knew it was time to get the hell out of there, and so I did."

In every way this seemed victory enough for her. Just to get away from someone before it was too late.

"The thing is, if I can get another chance, I can get out of LA," she said.

"Where would you go?"

"Colorado, I think."

"Why Colorado?"

"I don't know. Big-sky country."

Her eyes darted about.

She was looking for something else to talk about. Idly, in a way that was completely off-hand, she reached over to the dash, where she'd put the photograph Simon had given me the night before.

"What's this?"

She gave it a quick once-over, then froze, her gaze fixed on the photograph. She looked as if she'd just picked up a rattlesnake.

As if to conceal whatever had just happened in her mind, she returned the picture to the dash.

"What was in the picture?" I asked.

"Nothing." She took a quick, nervous pull on the cigarette.

"You ever been to Colorado?" she asked, a shift I recognized as purely a diversion.

She wanted nothing more than to change the subject, but that wasn't going to happen.

I looked at her sternly. "What did you see in that picture, Destiny?"

"Nothing," she repeated.

I knew this wasn't true.

"Now's not the time to lie to me," I warned her.

She was scared again, looking for a way out.

"I can't," she said. "Vicki would kill me." She was terrified. "I can't. I can't."

I nodded toward the picture. There was only one man she could have recognized. I tapped Simon's smiling face. "You know who he is?"

She shook her head, but I saw the truth in her eyes.

"You've seen him, haven't you?"

She hesitated briefly, but she was cornered.

"You've seen this man," I said firmly.

She nodded.

"At the farmhouse?" I asked.

She nodded again. "Yes."

I plucked the picture from the dash and held it before her.

"Are you sure?" I demanded.

She looked at the picture like a witness picking a face out of a lineup.

"It was him."

If this was true, I thought, everything Claire had ever said was accurate. All her accusations.

About her father in the past.

About Simon in the present.

I glanced at the photograph that had fixed Destiny's gaze.

Smiling Simon.

My father erect in his uniform, looking as firm as his convictions.

The simple fact that they were in the same photograph struck me as an obscenity.

The whole idea of the scholarship in my father's name had never been anything but a ploy to win me over. And I'd fallen for it.

What a fool I must seem to Simon Miller, I said to myself. *Merely another woman who fell into his trap.*

CLAIRE

IT IS NEARLY six when I get home.

I sit down in the chair in the foyer and try to absorb the fact that my father is near the end.

A car horn sounds outside. A short burst, like someone being summoned. Then another and another. Quick little beeps. Every five seconds. I try to ignore it, but the beeps keep coming. Harsh. Rapid. Maddening. It's like being repeatedly jabbed in the ear.

I get up, walk to the window, and look out.

There he is.

Mehdi.

Sitting in his car, staring at my house, grinning each time he beeps his horn. He has a smug superiority on his face. He thinks I'm defenseless against his petty harassment.

But I'm not.

A rage lifts me and carries me to the desk.

I unlock the drawer.

Max's pistol rests motionless, inert, unthreatening, until I yank it from its long sleep.

Mehdi's eyes widen as I burst through the door.

Instantly he sees the pistol, turns, and reaches for the ignition.

But I surge forward, as if carried on the wind.

I am at his car, pressing the barrel of Max's revolver against his temple. "Put your hands on the wheel!" I command him.

He pales instantly.

In my cold eyes he reads his death warrant.

"Claire, it was just a joke—just a joke. I—"

"Put your hands on the wheel!"

My voice peals through the failing light.

"Do it!"

Mehdi is sputtering.

"Just a joke, Claire—those bad reviews! I'll take them back. I promise."

I press the barrel hard against the side of his head.

"Shut up."

"Claire, please, I—"

"Shut up!"

I jerk back the hammer.

The sound of its metal click hits Mehdi like an electric shock. His body goes rigid, then almost immediately limp.

"Please, Claire."

He begins to whimper.

I look at him evenly. "Don't ever come here again."

I ease the pistol away from his head.

He quickly hits the ignition and races away.

As he leaves, I feel the heft of the pistol in my hand. Its power reverberates up my arm and into my brain.

I watch as Mehdi's car disappears around a far corner.

As he vanishes, I am seized by the simple thought of how easy it is to stop a man.

All you have to do is accept the consequences.

SLOAN

I WASTED NO time calling Simon.

"I've learned a few things," I said when he answered the phone. Very pointedly, I added, "About Claire."

"Oh?"

"We should go for a drive."

"You mean now? Tonight?"

"We shouldn't wait."

Simon heard the warning in my voice and assumed that Claire was about to fly off the handle again.

"I see," he said solemnly. "All right."

I'd already picked a place not far from the Palazzo and told him to meet me there.

He arrived a few minutes later, dressed for a casual dinner in LA: yellow Lacoste polo, blue shorts.

"Where we headed?" he asked as he got into my car.

"Out of town."

"Why?"

"We have to be careful."

He looked pleased and seemed to think that I'd reached the point he'd been urging me toward all along.

"You plan to do something, don't you?" he asked. "About Claire."

I nodded.

He was silent for a time, thinking very seriously.

"That stuff you told Claire about knowing people. Is that true? Do you really know people like that?"

The question didn't strike me as simply making conversation. I suspected that killing Claire was emerging as Plan B.

"Yes," I said.

"Wouldn't that be a twist in the story?" he asked in a way that suggested just how much it amused him. "Claire the one who ends up dead instead of Evil Simon."

He was perfectly relaxed with me now.

"Have you ever been out this way?" I asked as I turned onto the road that led to the farmhouse.

Miller shook his head.

A while later we reached the house. The yellow beams of my headlights illuminated its blackened windows and red door. Simon examined the place without expression.

"It was a brothel," I said.

Miller shrugged.

"Boys will be boys."

"The girls were underage," I added.

Simon remained silent, unruffled.

I was looking for a sign that he knew the house, was a regular client, but he gave no indication of ever having been here.

At the same time, he asked nothing about why I'd driven him into the desert, stopped at this desolate place.

Instead he made an assumption.

"You're hatching something, aren't you? That's why we're here. To discuss it."

He laughed.

"You have a flair for the dramatic, Sloan."

He glanced about.

"Very cinematic, a location like this. Sets the mood, right?"

He was like a little boy enjoying a game.

"Let's go inside," I said.

We both got out of the car and walked toward the house. A little breeze played over the desert floor. It gently rocked the sagebrush and rustled through the dry grass.

A long line of stairs led up to a wide, sagging porch. The creaks that sounded beneath our feet were like tiny cries.

I opened the door of the farmhouse and motioned Simon into the front room. He walked to the back window, opened it, and peered out. There was nothing but emptiness beyond it.

"It's peaceful out here," he said. "I've considered buying a place in the desert."

He strode to the center of the room and made

a slow turn. The look on his face was harder that any I'd seen before. Something had changed, but I didn't know what it was. He seemed more aggressive and self-assured, like an unarmed man who suddenly grabs a gun.

"You'd have been commissioner one day if you'd stayed with the LAPD," he told me. "Your father didn't make it, but you would have." He began a circular stroll around the room, his hands behind him, completely nonchalant. "You know what it's called, this house?" he asked.

He saw how much his question surprised me.

"Lolitaville," he said nostalgically, like a man remembering good times. "Funny how things change, Sloan. Back in the day, the age of consent for girls was ten. And I don't mean marriage. I mean sexual consent."

"We're not living back in the day," I reminded him.

He stopped his tour of the room and faced me.

"It's been going on out here for years," he said. "At this house. Because we found someone to protect it. Someone who knew the ropes. Someone in law enforcement."

His gaze went cold.

"Someone who was ambitious. Who wanted to be commissioner." He smiled. "I'm sure you know a man like that."

And there it was. The reason for his self-assurance.

"My father protected Lolitaville?" I asked. "Is that what you're saying?"

The polite, modest, falsely accused Simon fell away like a mask he no longer needed.

"Do you think I'm stupid, Sloan?" he asked evenly.

He stared at me scornfully.

"Do you think I didn't catch on to what this was all about the minute we headed out this way?"

He chuckled lightly. It was all just a game to him, one whose rules he knew well and could faithfully depend upon.

"Why do you think I called you that day, Sloan?" he asked. "Of all the fixers, cleaners, sin eaters, or whatever you call yourselves, in LA, why you? It's because I had a hook in you. A way of controlling you."

He was utterly certain that he was beyond my power to touch him.

"You know what your trouble is, Sloan?" he asked. "You're still Daddy's little girl. You want your father to be a victim. A man lied about and destroyed by a crazy bitch. You don't want anything to ever tarnish that image."

He grinned.

"Am I right?"

When I didn't answer, he walked to the far corner of the room and leaned against the wall.

"But if I go down, so does your sainted father," he said.

His gaze was cold and confident, that of a man who knew where the secrets were and how to expose them to the world.

"Because everything your mother believed about him was true."

He abruptly straightened himself and headed for the door.

"Can we go back to LA now?" he asked. "Charlotte and Emma are waiting for me."

He turned and strode out onto the porch.

I followed him and closed the door.

He strutted across the porch toward the steps. When he reached the top of them, he took a deep, pleasurable breath.

"I do love the desert air," he said.

He lifted his gaze to the stars. His expression was relaxed and unafraid. "I'm a bit of an ornithologist," he said. "Did you know that swallows live eighty percent of their lives in the air? They eat in flight, and gather the materials for their nests. They even mate in flight. Imagine that."

He laughed.

"It gives new meaning to sex on the fly, don't you think?"

He reached the edge of the porch, then wheeled around.

"Don't worry about your dad," he told me,

almost soothingly. "His reputation is safe with me."

The darkness that surrounded us seemed limitless and impenetrable, a black oblivion that blocked every source of light save for the flash of Simon's sneering grin.

"You're a liar," I said.

Simon smiled. "Maybe. But you'll never know, will you? Unless you look into the history of this place. Which you won't. Because you're afraid of what you'll find."

He was daring me to investigate my own father, and he was certain I wouldn't. He'd stained my father's memory in my mind, and he knew it would remain that way. I would look no further into his accusation for fear of discovering that everything I'd ever admired in the man—his goodness, his incorruptibility—was a lie.

When I simply stared at Simon, he stepped back. A little creak sounded a plaintive plea beneath his feet of a small thing breaking.

I remembered that Claire's passionate hope had been for something "out there" to stop men like Simon Miller. I thought, *This is what would happen:*

A board would give way.

Simon would lose his footing and somersault down the stairs, head to wood, head to wood, repeatedly and violently, until he sprawled in the dust at the bottom of them.

He would die like this unless something out there intervened to stop him.

But the only thing out there was me.

And I did nothing but watch as Simon turned and walked, undeterred, down the stairs.

CLAIRE

I WATCH THE sun rise after a sleepless night. It dawns pink and gold, but nothing is beautiful to me anymore.

Even daybreak is an indictment, because Simon's wedding day moves relentlessly forward.

Last night it infected my dreams. Simon stands in a dark corridor, with Emma at the other end. I am between them, watching as Simon takes first one step, then another. He is sure that I will retreat as he closes in on Emma.

I awoke thinking of the pistol.

After chasing Mehdi away, I placed it on the night table beside my bed.

It was the first thing I saw in the morning light.

I thought of Mehdi's sputtering panic, how petrified he'd been, though I'd never had any attention of actually shooting him.

Simon is not like Mehdi. Mehdi is a pathetic little coward. Simon is a force only death can stop.

Only death.

I imagine the gun in my hand.

In my dream, Simon takes another step down the corridor.

I draw the pistol.

He smiles and takes another step.

I raise the gun.

His smile broadens.

I pull the trigger.

Simon stumbles back like a villain in a film noir, a swath of black blood spreading over his chest.

It's only a movie image, but it feels absolutely real.

SLOAN

I GOT TO work at just after nine the next morning. Jake was already in his office. He took one look at me and guessed that I'd had a rough night.

"Jesus, Sloan," he said, "you look like hell."

I sat down in the chair in front of his desk.

"Have you ever heard of a place called Lolitaville?" I asked.

He shook his head.

"A house out in the desert. Where girls were taken. Young girls. Someone told me that back in the day, an LA cop protected it. I want to know if that's true."

Jake stared at me suspiciously.

"Why would it matter now, Sloan?"

"I just want to know."

He thought a moment, then said, "Well, bad cops know who the other bad cops are, so you should probably start there."

"Who should I ask?"

"I'd talk to Nick Devine," Jake answered. "He was as dirty as they get. And I hear he has cancer. Just a few months to live. He might be willing to talk, since he has nothing to lose."

Nick Devine, I thought. *Of all people.*

CLAIRE

MY FIRST CLIENT of the morning is Ray Patrick, but I don't want to see him. Suspicion has clouded everything. Why did he hire me under false pretenses?

I think of the young girl Ray was speaking with at the gallery, her adoring gaze. Simon had loved it when Melody looked at him that way.

Does an adolescent's gushing admiration have the same effect on Ray?

I glance toward the parking lot.

Ray will arrive at any minute.

I consider leaving, because my mind has been completely poisoned by mistrust.

I am still wrestling with that thought when a black SUV pulls into the parking lot. Is it the one that followed me before?

I wait for the driver to get out.

It's Ray.

He stands, waiting, until a young girl comes around from the other side of the car. He takes her hand and they come into the coffee shop where I am waiting.

"Hi, Claire," Ray says when he reaches my table. "This is my daughter, Jade. She's been wanting to learn a little French."

She has Down syndrome.

My heart melts at her smile.

"I wanted to make sure you were a good match for her," Ray tells me, then adds in French, "*Désolé de vous avoir induite en erreur*." He is sorry for misleading me.

The weight of doubting Ray, along with all my dark suspicions about him, suddenly drops from me.

He smiles. "By the way, how's my accent?"

"Your accent is perfect," I assure him.

"I hope you don't mind my deceiving you a little, but I know how important it is to have the right match. I'm sure you and Jade will like each other."

"I'm sure we will."

"Then why don't we start her first lesson now?"

"Okay."

Ray waits at a distance while I have my class with Jade.

"Thank you, Claire," he says at the end of the lesson.

He looks at me closely.

"Are you all right?" he asks.

I avoid the question. "Where did you learn French?" I ask.

"I lived in Paris when I was a young man with artistic aspirations but no talent to justify them," Ray answers in that tone of self-mockery I find appealing. "It was my year of living dangerously.

I would like to live there again someday, but I promise not to paint."

He pauses, then adds quite seriously, "I don't want to go there alone."

Is he asking me to envision the two of us in Paris? It's a possibility I can't entertain, because I know it's not going to happen. I have accepted the only road open to me now, and it does not lead to Paris.

Which is why, when I left my house this morning, I took Max's gun.

SLOAN

NICK DEVINE WASN'T hard to find. Since retiring from the LAPD he'd spent his days slouched in a shadowy corner of the Home Plate Bar, nursing a whiskey and regaling his drinking buddies with tales of life on the job.

Cancer had thinned him slightly, and he looked more worn, but the sinister twinkle in his eyes remained the same. He'd lived his life as a rogue cop, and nothing in that slimy past in the least bothered him. He was as shameless as they come, a man who'd never once reproached himself for the dirty things he'd done. For Devine, corruption was the way of the world, and he hadn't offered the slightest resistance to it.

When he saw me, he waved halfheartedly, with no indication of inviting me to join him at his table.

"Detective Wilson," he said when I did it anyway. "I didn't think you ever came here. Figured it was too blue for you."

"Blue?"

"Too many cops."

"I was a cop."

"*Was* being the operative word."

He could tell I had something on my mind, but

he looked surprised when I said, "You were with the old Vice Squad, right?"

He laughed at the very word.

"Vice? What's that? Nothing but victimless crimes. Making a bet. Loaning money at a higher rate than some bank that wouldn't loan you a dime in the first place. Where's the vice in that?"

This was boilerplate Nick Devine, and under less pressing circumstances I would simply have gotten up and walked away. But as Jake said, bad cops know bad cops, and if my father was the man Simon had described, Devine would know about it.

He went on in this vein for a few minutes. The usual stories about finding stars caught with hookers, often of the same sex. He threw in a car chase here and a stakeout there. He scoffed at honor and made light of anyone who believed in it.

It wasn't long until I was fed up.

"Tell me about Lolitaville," I said.

Devine's dancing eyes grew still.

"Why are you interested?" he asked.

"I have a client who's been . . . implicated," I told him. "I'm trying to drag him clear of it."

He was quiet for a few seconds, thinking it over.

"Hell, I'm dying," he said finally. "The doc says I got about a month. Why should I care who knows what?"

He cocked his head to the right.

"What do you want to know, Detective?"

"Anything you can tell me," I said.

"It was a whorehouse out in the sticks," Devine answered. "Bigwigs used it. Movie-mogul types. Fancy-pants lawyers and politicians. Which always struck me as strange, because they could have afforded the best. Top-flight whores. Luxury hotels. But this bunch, they liked it down and dirty. It was part of the thrill, I guess, to be in a crummy house in the middle of nowhere."

He nodded to the NO SMOKING sign at the far end of the room, then pointedly took out a cigarette and lit it. "In cop bars, I can do whatever I want and nobody says squat."

He had the voice of a dead man walking, at last free of all restraint.

"Who runs the place now?" I asked.

"It's closed for now, I hear, but it'll probably start up again after a while. It's run by a bottom-feeding whore named Vicki Page. As evil a bitch as God ever made."

He leaned back, fully relaxed. He might have been in a chaise longue by the pool, taking in the sun.

"Why did it close?" I asked.

He shrugged.

"My guess is Vicki felt some heat, so she closed it to be safe. She's done it before. When a girl escaped and couldn't be found for a while, or somebody came snooping around. Anytime she thought it might be found out, she'd shut it down until things cooled. That's the way Vicki operates. You get close, she folds the tent and disappears into the night. But it'll be up and running again once the smoke clears."

He was obviously well acquainted with the operation.

"Was it always called Lolitaville?" I asked.

"No. It only got that name a few years ago." Devine answered as freely as he might have responded to the questions of a census taker. "When the clientele's taste changed from well-done to rare."

"What does that mean?"

"They wanted young stuff."

"I see."

"Vicki was more than happy to oblige, of course," Devine said. "Her morals would gag a maggot."

So would Devine's, I thought, but I kept it to myself and went on to the next question. "Where did—"

"Wait a minute," Devine interrupted. "I been telling you stuff. How about I get some answers from you?"

"Okay."

"Where you'd hear about Lolitaville?"

"From Simon Miller."

The name clearly caught Devine by surprise.

"What do you have to do with Simon Miller?" he asked.

"He's a client."

We were both saying things we shouldn't, which suggested that we were on an equal footing. By revealing my client's name, I assured Devine that I trusted him to keep his mouth shut, so he could trust me to do the same.

A malicious delight came into Devine's eyes.

"You're doing Simon Miller's dirty work?" he asked.

"It's a living," I answered drily.

Devine flung his arm over the back of his seat.

"Well, I'll be damned," he muttered.

He blew a line of smoke directly toward me. His smile was all self-satisfaction.

"You really are a chip off the old block, Sloan."

I pretended that remark had no effect upon me.

"What do you mean?" I asked.

Devine took a long pull on the cigarette and sent another blast of smoke in my direction.

"Hell-bent to get ahead," he answered. "A real hot dog. Convinced you got all the right stuff. Just like your father was."

He looked faintly puzzled.

"You were moving up fast in the department just like him," he told me. "Then you up and quit. Why'd you do that?"

"I had trouble with the life," I answered. "Trouble being a good cop."

"Your father had trouble with that, too," Devine said.

He threw back his head and laughed.

"The incorruptible Monroe Wilson."

The way he mouthed my father's name seemed seeded with a foul implication.

"My father didn't have trouble being a good cop," I said insistently. "Which is what made it unfair."

"Made what unfair?"

"The stuff my mother said about him. That he was corrupt."

Devine drew a final puff on his cigarette. "A gutsy woman, your mom."

"Gutsy?" I said derisively. "Does it take guts to lie about a man? Destroy his career? It doesn't take guts to defame a good man."

"Maybe your mother didn't think he was good," Devine said.

"You think she actually believed what she said about him?"

"I'm just saying that if you once believed a man was good, it would hit hard to find out that you were wrong. You'd been played for a fool. A man that you thought you knew and that you really admired wasn't admirable at all. He was just another liar. Another hypocrite. Another dirty cop."

His gaze seemed almost as tinged with pain as my mother's had been. "My wife was disappointed in me, too," he told me.

He was suddenly quite weary.

"I guess there's nothing lower than a fallen god," he added.

"But my father wasn't a—"

Devine silenced me with a wave of his hand.

"Anyway, it's water under the bridge. Forget it."

"Forget it? How? She destroyed him. I can't forget that. Or forgive her for it."

Devine shrugged.

"She was dangerous to have around, that's for sure. Pointing her finger. Claiming she had evidence."

"She didn't claim to have evidence," I reminded him.

"Oh, yes she did," Devine said.

His smile was almost playful, but the tone of his voice was dead serious. "She was going to hand it over to Harry Griggs."

"Harry Griggs?"

"Harry was the head of Internal Affairs in those days," Devine explained. "Always wore white linen suits with a matching hat. That's why they called him White Hat Harry."

He was utterly confident about his view of the world. That it was ugly and malicious and that no one really stood for anything.

"Your mother was set to spill the beans to Harry."

He crushed what was left of his cigarette onto the tabletop.

"Well, you know what happened after that," he said.

He thumped out another cigarette and lit it.

"Which was very fortunate for your dad, of course."

His eyes narrowed knowingly.

"Very, very fortunate."

He smiled, and I felt the full thrust of his implication.

"Because your mother was . . . an inconvenient woman."

He winked.

"The type you need to get rid of," he continued, with no effort to conceal the shocking thing he was suggesting. "If you want to get ahead."

This was Nick Devine at his sleaziest, a creature of dark innuendo alluding to ghastly things.

I didn't buy it.

"The LAPD did a full investigation," I reminded him. "My mother committed suicide. Every report came to the same conclusion. From the coroner on up."

A smile slithered back onto Devine's lips.

"Well, that's the thing about suicide," he said. "Especially with a gun to the head. It's easy to fake. You make sure the body is in the right position and the pistol is in the right place. You add a little carbon residue here and there."

He shrugged.

"Easy."

His eyes were knife points.

"You'd know how to fake a suicide like that, wouldn't you, Sloan?" he asked almost teasingly.

"Yes."

"Where did you learn that particular skill?"

"On the job."

He released a long, slow breath.

"Just like your old man."

He was doing it again, insinuating that my father had faked my mother's suicide.

"My father wasn't in the house when it happened," I told him firmly. "He was at head-quarters. I found my mother."

"Yes, I know," Devine said. "You were supposed to be home by three thirty, but you were late."

"How do you know that?"

"How do you think I know it?"

"Anyone could have told you."

He seemed hardly to hear me.

"It was supposed to be a murder-suicide thing," he said evenly. "That way no one would question it. A mother kills her daughter, then herself. A case like that, it's cut and dried.

Everybody knows the crazy mother did it. There usually isn't even much of an investigation. At least, not the sort of investigation there'd be if it was only your mother who'd died."

I laughed in his face.

"So my father hired you to kill my mother and me?"

Devine didn't laugh. He stared at me silently.

"You need a better story," I said contemptuously. "I mean, come on, Nick, do you really expect me to believe any of this?"

Something in him softened, as if he'd been taken up by a malign nostalgia. "You were wearing a cute little red dress when you came home that day," he said.

I stared at him coolly.

"The back door was supposed to be open, remember?" Devine asked. "But it was locked, and so you went around to the front."

I felt my skin tighten around my bones.

"You were a very sweet-looking little girl, Sloan," he added almost gently. "Innocent."

He seemed to see me again as I'd been that day. Seven years old. A child.

"I went out the back as you came in the front. End of story."

When I said nothing, he added in a tone that was almost intimate, "I'll burn in hell for things I've done. But at least I couldn't do that." He shook his head. "Not even for the incorruptible Monroe Wilson."

I felt a hole in the earth.

It opened beneath me.

I fell and fell.

CLAIRE

THE CALL COMES in just before noon.

A doctor tells me that my father is dying.

I drive to the hospital.

He is lying on his back, eyes closed, breathing very lightly, releasing gentle puffs of air. Mine is a death watch, nothing more.

It ends an hour later, when his breathing stops. I summon a nurse, then do the paperwork necessary for the removal and cremation of his body.

I am numb.

I feel nothing.

I am focused only on the next three hours.

By that time, if Simon follows his normal schedule, he will be home.

"There's a chaplain, if you want to see him," a kindly hospital clerk tells me when I sign the last of the papers. "And we can provide a grief counselor."

I shake my head.

"No, thank you."

Before leaving, I walk down the corridor to Margot's room. An old woman is now in what had been her bed.

I go to the nurses' station.

A young man is working at a computer.

"Can you tell me what happened to Margot Garrett? She was in Room 414."

"Let me check."

He types a few strokes.

"Are you a relative?"

"No. Her French teacher."

"Well, I'm sorry to tell you, but Mrs. Garrett passed away early this morning."

It was a death I might have prevented. It eliminates any further doubts as to what I have to do.

I turn and head toward my car.

I promise myself that I will never act too late again.

Nothing will stop me now.

SLOAN

SIMON'S VOICE CAME through clear and crisp: *But you'll never know, will you? Unless you look. Which you won't.*

But I had looked.

Now I had to deal with what I'd found.

I turned off the tape and sat in the stony silence of my office.

During the next few minutes I searched for a way out of the windowless cell I was locked in, and wondered how I might ever be released from it.

There seemed only one key: to take up and hold . . . the feather.

I pocketed the tape and went to my car.

CLAIRE

I ARRIVE TO offer my last hour of French.

"*Bonjour*," Chloé says cheerfully when she opens the door.

"*Bonjour.*"

She leads me to a table where she's already arranged the book for the class.

I point to a drawing of people standing in a snowy park, wrapped in heavy coats and scarves. "*Il fait . . . ?*"

"*Froid*," Chloé responds delightedly. Cold.

I point to a scene of people on the beach, a bright sun above them. "*Il fait . . . ?*"

"*Chaud.*" Hot.

The third drawing is of a little girl standing in front of a large house. She wears a huge smile. "*Elle est . . . ?*"

"*Heureuse.*" Happy.

"*Très bien*," I tell Chloé, because she has correctly used the feminine form of the adjective.

The next picture shows the same little girl, her eyes moist, her smile now a frown. "*Elle est . . . ?*"

"*Triste.*"

"*Super.*"

In the final drawing, a different little girl stands

at the door of a house that somewhat resembles Simon's. "*Elle est . . . ?*"

Chloé gives the right answer. "*A la porte.*" At the door.

I peer at the drawing of the little girl and think of Emma. *Elle est en danger*, I say to myself in French. She is in danger.

Then I tell myself in English, *But not for long.*

SLOAN

CANDACE LOOKED AT me somberly as she turned off the tape.

"Miller didn't think you'd come after him," she said. "Not at the risk of damaging your father's reputation."

I'd already told her about the warning I'd gotten from Vicki Page and the much more disturbing talk I'd had with Nick Devine, save for the final moments I'd spent with him. The last of his awful accusations were still echoing through my mind, but I kept them to myself.

"There'll have to be an investigation, Sloan," Candace said ominously. "A very thorough one."

She meant an official inquiry that could unearth a world of corruption in which my father might have been involved.

"I know," I told her.

She saw the pain in my eyes.

"Is there something else, Sloan?" she asked.

I shook my head.

"Not at the moment."

"Well, don't worry, we'll bring Simon Miller to justice," she assured me.

I wanted to give Claire the same confident assurance. I reached for my phone and dialed her number.

CLAIRE

AS I DRIVE, I think of that final night with Melody. I see her once again on the rainy deck, peering out over the darkly churning water as I approach her. I hear our conversation, my last words to her still the most searing: *I don't believe you.*

The circle is complete.

I didn't believe Melody, and now no one believes me.

Except for Sloan.

Which no longer matters.

It's up to me. Only me.

I compare my life to Emma's.

She is a child, with everything before her. I am forty-four. Childless. Alone. The life I'll lose is nothing compared to the one she'll lose if I don't act.

I look all around. Everything is distant and silent. Los Angeles has been reduced to a static background, like a projection in film, a mere image on a screen.

Time, too, has stopped. It's as surreal as a Dali painting. All the clocks have melted.

My cell phone rings, but I don't answer it.

I'm no longer just a woman. I'm a bullet hurtling toward its target.

344

SLOAN

WHEN CLAIRE DIDN'T answer her phone, I looked at my GPS.

She was on the road, as she usually was, driving from one client to another.

But as I followed the blinking light that located her on the LA street map and watched as she made one turn, then another, I saw exactly where she was headed.

Simon's house.

I snapped up my phone and called her again.

No answer.

I looked at the GPS map.

She was only a few miles away.

Simon had mentioned a gun. I immediately visualized it in her hand.

I knew I'd put it there with my talk of murder. She was following a direction I'd given her.

I glanced again at the GPS. There was no doubt that she was trained on Simon. I had no time to think or plan.

I rushed for my car. *Stop, Claire,* I thought desperately. *You don't have to do this.*

CLAIRE

MY CELL RINGS again as I pull into the driveway of Simon's house.

I have not been here since my breakdown.

It looks the same as it did that day.

I tuck the pistol into my handbag and head for the door.

On my way, I envision myself reaching for it, firing it, Simon's body stumbling backward and falling heavily in the foyer.

I cannot imagine anything after that.

I arrive at the door and ring the bell.

When I hear footsteps, I place my finger on the trigger.

I'll say nothing to Simon.

I won't give him time to say anything to me.

The instant the door opens, I'll kill him.

The footsteps halt.

He is just behind the door.

I hear the latch.

The door opens.

SLOAN

I CHECKED CLAIRE'S tracking.

The little blue ball that was her car had stopped. She was at Simon's house.

I swerved to the right and weaved through the traffic, honking madly as I pumped the accelerator.

It was LA. Cars were everywhere, blocking every route, clogging the veins of the city.

My only weapon was my horn, so I pounded it mercilessly, as if expecting Claire to hear it and realize that I was coming to save her from doing something no longer necessary.

I heard Candace's voice again, assuring me that Simon Miller was going down. It was over for Claire. Her long nightmare.

I picked up the phone and dialed her number again.

CLAIRE

MY PHONE RINGS, but Charlotte gives no indication that she hears it.

She stands rigidly at the door.

"Hello, Claire," she says.

Her voice is steady, without fear. There is none of the panic or anger of our last meeting. She makes no move to close the door.

"I came to see Simon," I tell her. "I'll come back another time."

With that, I turn to leave.

"He's here," Charlotte says.

She steps from the doorway to let me in.

"Come in."

There is a strange look in her eyes.

I shake my head. "No, I'll—"

"Come in, Claire," she interrupts commandingly.

I fear I'm the victim of an ambush she and Simon have set for me.

I reach into my bag and grip the pistol.

"He's waiting for you," she says as she motions me inside.

My phone rings again as she escorts me down the corridor.

I expect it to stop after a few rings, but it's still pealing through the air when we enter Simon's office.

SLOAN

THERE WAS STILL no answer.

I saw a break in the traffic and sped forward.

I was in Simon's neighborhood now. Wider streets. Less traffic.

I pressed down hard on the accelerator and my car bolted forward like a racing horse at the bell.

I glanced at the GPS.

Arrival time: 10:37.

It was 10:34.

CLAIRE

"THERE'S SIMON," CHARLOTTE says as I follow her into the office.

I expect to see him seated grandly behind his large mahogany desk, but instead Charlotte nods toward the floor.

Simon is lying on his back, like a body floating faceup in water. There is a hole on the right side of his head, and his hair is soaked in blood.

Charlotte gives me a few seconds to stare at Simon's body.

"Something was wrong with Emma," she begins. "I noticed it when he brought her home last night."

She folds her arms over her chest and presses back against the wall as if in need of its support.

"I asked her about it, and she told me that Simon made her feel . . . uncomfortable."

She has been staring at Simon's body. Now her gaze drifts over to me.

"I came here to talk to him," she continues. "He said it was all in Emma's mind and I was stupid to listen to her."

She draws in a deep, trembling breath.

" 'You're just like Claire,' he said. 'As insane as she is.' "

Her eyes drift to Simon.

"He took a gun out of his desk. This was for our protection, he told me. Because he was afraid of what you might do."

"What *I* might do?"

Charlotte nods. "To me or Emma."

Her voice goes cold.

"He took the pistol and put it in my hand and pressed the barrel against the side of his head. He said, 'If you believe your daughter, shoot me.'"

This was the Simon I knew. Always the star of his own big show.

He tightened his grip on my hand and pressed the barrel of the pistol even harder against his head. 'Go ahead,' he said. 'Shoot.'"

I can see Simon enjoying every minute of it.

"He put my finger on the trigger," Charlotte goes on. "He said, 'Well, do you believe Emma or not?'"

She stares at me plaintively. "I couldn't move."

I imagined a triumphant glint in Simon's eyes. He was winning, and he'd known it.

"When I didn't move, he said to me, 'Don't ever accuse me again, Charlotte.' His voice was really hard. He was a king giving orders to a servant. *'And don't ever stand in my way. Because I always get what I want.'*" She looks at me appreciatively.

"That's when I remembered the last thing you said to me, Claire: *'Believe your daughter.'*"

She glances at Simon's body before her gaze returns to me.

"I believed my daughter. I pulled the trigger."

For the first time Charlotte seems almost to crumble.

"I don't know what to do now, Claire."

I'm about to console her when I hear another voice.

"I do."

I turn toward the door. Sloan is standing there. It's clear she's heard everything.

"I know what to do," she tells us. "You can both leave. Don't ever talk about this to anybody. And never contact me again."

She looks at me directly.

"Goodbye, Claire," is all she says.

THREE MONTHS LATER

CLAIRE

MY FIRST CLIENT of the day is a retired engineer named Mike. Both his parents were victims of Alzheimer's. By the time they were in their midsixties, they no longer recognized him. Mike is now fifty-nine and fears that he will soon be stricken, too. He has read that learning a language reduces the chances of contracting the disease.

He wishes only to memorize, so my lesson is designed to test and extend this particular skill. I say a French word and give him the English meaning. I do this five times, then test him. When he gets all five, he breaks out in a huge smile.

After Mike there is another and another, each a separate beat in the rhythm of my day.

By early evening I am back at home. I turn on the television. I have no interest in watching the Femme Fatale Network anymore. I no longer have anything in common with those movie-mayhem women.

I live in a very different world.

More open to possibility.

A world without Simon.

It's a life composed of nothing more dramatic than the carrying out of routine chores—preparing lessons, tidying up, cooking. I teach my clients, have lunch with Ava and dinner with Ray and Jade.

It's a simple life.

Precious.

I sometimes have the impression that I am living in the epilogue of my own story, quietly observing the final tying-up of its various threads.

Three days after Simon's death, the girl in the water was identified as Lily Robinson. An autopsy revealed that she'd died of a drug overdose. Vicki Page immediately came under suspicion, because by then Destiny was talking to the police, telling them that she'd taken Lily to Lolitaville. She'd also seen Lily's painting on the wall near McDuffy's. Her clear suggestion was that Vicki had ordered Lily's murder because she'd seen it, too. In response, the authorities put the squeeze on a number of Vicki's hired thugs. One of them confessed.

Lily was fifteen years old, an orphan. There were no known relatives. Her paintings now hang in the foyer of my house.

I don't see Destiny anymore, because she is in some version of protective custody. She was granted immunity in exchange for her testimony against Vicki Page, who has since been charged with Lily's murder as well as child trafficking. She is awaiting trial in the Los Angeles jail. Destiny has identified two men as having gone to Lolitaville, but Vicki, because she is facing life imprisonment and is now angling for a lighter sentence, has named many more. Almost by the week others are arrested. Doctors. Judges. Actors. Producers.

Because several LAPD cops were connected to Vicki's desert brothel, the press has dubbed the entire matter the "Lolitaville scandal." Several police officials have been exposed for protecting it over many years. The most prominent of them is Monroe Wilson.

I saw Sloan only once after Simon's death.

By accident.

I was with Jade on Santa Monica Pier, waiting for Ray to join us.

Sloan was at the far end, leaning on the railing, peering out to sea. What a lonely warrior she seemed. I wanted to go up to her, but I remembered her stern warning and turned away.

Goodbye, Sloan.

The small exhibition Ray gave of Lily's work opened to a modest group of gallery regulars, along with a few of his friends.

Ava came, as did a couple of people I'd met during my time at the auction house.

The only real surprise was Charlotte, who wisely kept her distance most of the time, though just before leaving she'd felt it safe to approach me.

"Emma's doing fine," she said. "I wanted you to know that."

We gave no indication of the secret we shared.

"Are you okay, Claire?" she asked.

"Yes, I am."

I thought of the "suicide" Sloan had competently staged, removing the surveillance tapes, arranging Simon's body, placing the pistol at just the right distance and angle for a self-inflicted wound, even providing the motive, which was that Sloan, who was, after all, Simon's sin eater, had informed him of an impending investigation into a desert brothel known as Lolitaville. Simon had reacted calmly, she'd told the first LAPD cops to arrive, and so she'd left him in his office, quite convinced that he was fine. She'd nearly reached the front door of the house when she'd heard the shot, then rushed back to find him dead. As a story, it was airtight.

Toward the end of the evening, I walked into the room where Ray had hung Lily's paintings. The sign at the entrance read: LILY'S WORLD. The paintings were framed in black and illuminated by a subdued light.

Ray came in and stood beside me. "Do you like the exhibit?" he asked.

"It's beautiful, Ray."

"Do you want to have dinner tonight?"

"I'd love to."

"Okay, I'll pick you up after I close the gallery."

"Is that too late to bring Jade?"

Ray shook his head. "No, it'll be the three of us."

The three of us.

How simple it now seems—happiness.

After leaving the gallery, I drove back home with the windows open. The warm rush of night air reminded me of an art festival I'd come across several years before. I'd noticed the portrait of a woman. She had been bound, but she was pulling free of her chains. Her head was tilted skyward and her arms were outstretched, feathers sprouting from them, becoming wings, lifting her from struggle, betrayal, doubt, pain, fear.

If it were that easy, we would all be soaring birds.

But just because it isn't easy doesn't mean it can't be done.

Center Point Large Print
600 Brooks Road / PO Box 1
Thorndike, ME 04986-0001 USA

(207) 568-3717

US & Canada:
1 800 929-9108
www.centerpointlargeprint.com